Elizabeth Amelia Sharp

Sea-Music

An Anthology of Poems and Passages Descriptive of the Sea

Elizabeth Amelia Sharp

Sea-Music
An Anthology of Poems and Passages Descriptive of the Sea

ISBN/EAN: 9783744765350

Printed in Europe, USA, Canada, Australia, Japan

Cover: Foto ©Andreas Hilbeck / pixelio.de

More available books at **www.hansebooks.com**

SEA-MUSIC.

An Anthology of
Poems and Passages Descriptive of the Sea.

EDITED BY

MRS. WILLIAM SHARP,

Editor of " Women's Voices," " Great Musical Composers," &c.

" For I have loved thee, Ocean !"
BYRON.

LONDON:
WALTER SCOTT, 24, WARWICK LANE, E.C.

AND NEWCASTLE-ON-TYNE.

1887.

INDEX.

PREFATORY NOTE.

THE Sea has washed along the shores of many a dead and dying empire before and since the Greek poet spoke of "the multitudinous laughter of the ocean waves." The galleys of young nations have sailed over it to triumph and domination; the armadas of tottering kingdoms have been engulfed within its depths. Yet though the sea has been in all ages the highway of empire, it has been regarded by most of the generations of men as divorced from Nature as made manifest to us upon the Land. The Sea has always been a dread, a wonder; but—so far as we know—no peoples have loved it as in these latter days it is loved by us.

Of old it was ever the way of adventure, of discovery, of conquest; the girdle of safety; an unfathomable mystery, a terror, a desolation. But it was not loved till the world had become aweary with much thought, despair, and illusive hope: till the East and South had bowed submissively to the North. And among all northern races those with Celtic blood in their veins have most loved, feared, and worshipped the sea. Along the shores of Brittany, by the caves of Guernsey and Sark, where the Cornish cliffs and rocks continually withstand the onslaught of the Atlantic, along the wild coast-line of western Ireland, and around the greater part of the Scottish sea-board—there for long years have dwelt, and dwell, those to whom the sea is the supreme mystery and wonder of creation, the most ancient thing in the world, the secret keeper of the occult knowledge of the things of oblivion.

So late is the general awakening to the sea-magic that it may fairly be said to be a nineteenth-century characteristic. Before Byron and Shelley there was not much said or sung about the ocean, save incidental references such as have occurred in all literatures. In Shakespeare there is surprisingly little, fine as are the few passages which do occur in his songs and plays. And after Shakespeare till the advent of the

Romantic movement, how little there is of sea-description, of sea-love !

There is no doubt of the genuineness of Byron's love for the sea, though he was never affected by it so keenly as Shelley was. Wordsworth has endowed our literature with some splendid lines and passages, but he was at once too much of an inlander and an egoist to enter into the inheritance of the children of the Sea. The finest sea-music in English poetry has been echoed by poets of the Victorian era, by poets now living among us.

Mr. Swinburne, especially, has sung of the sea with an ardour and a delight which seem unflagging ; and the word itself is to be found in his poetry with a frequency probably exceeding that of its occurrence in the collective writings of all preceding English poets. Mr. Robert Buchanan, again, is noteworthy for his deep love and understanding of the sea: a true northerner, he more than any other contemporary poet betrays the magic of the Celtic glamour. Mr. Matthew Arnold and Lord Tennyson have written sea-strains that will endure for their beauty and insight. As to the quality of insight, Mr. Arnold comes nearer Heine than does any other English poet. Perhaps he too feels as strongly as did the sad, weary author of " Die Nordsee," when he wrote the exquisite little lyric beginning—

> Das Meer erstrahlt im Sonnenschein—

feels how good is intercommunion between transitory Man and the intransient Sea.

Perhaps no writer, either in prose or verse, has sufficiently emphasized the formative power of the sea in the development of human character. The sea's influence can mould a human being as its waves can mould the damp sand-dunes: as the mountaineer is always a mountaineer, so the children of the sea betray unmistakably, wheresoever they may be, at once their parentage and their lealty.

It is in poetry only we find that large ut-terance concerning the sea, which is so infinitely beyond any prose saying : such lines, for instance, as Keats'—

> " The moving waters at their priestlike task
> Of pure ablution round Earth's human shores."

Or the same poet's—

> " It keeps eternal whisperings around
> Desolate shores, and with its mighty swell
> Gluts twice ten thousand caverns."

In prose we have but one writer who has been

as much inspired by the magic of the sea as was Victor Hugo when he wrote "Les Travailleurs de la Mer"—Mr. Clark Russell, in whose *Golden Hope*, for instance, are passages of great descriptive beauty. Among those who have written prose descriptions of certain marine aspects, and of the "deep sea-meanings," Mr. Ruskin is supreme. For mere delineation of marine aspects, prose is superior to poetry. I am tempted to quote two passages, one from Mr. Ruskin's "Modern Painters," the other from a prose poem by Mr. Roden Noel ; each passage in exemplification of the exquisite detail in which the prosaist can fittingly indulge, a licence unpermitted to the writer in verse,—to the singer of the sea-song, the interpreter of the sea-lore, the prophet of its occult meanings and veiled prophecies.

"It is a sunset on the Atlantic after prolonged storm ; but the storm is partially lulled, and the torn and streaming rain-clouds are moving in scarlet lines to lose themselves in the hollow of the night. The whole surface of sea is divided into two ridges of enormous swell, not high, nor local, but a low, broad heaving of the whole ocean, like the lifting of its bosom by deep-drawn breath after the torture of the storm. Between these two ridges, the fire of the sunset falls along the trough of the sea, dyeing it with an awful but glorious light, the intense and lurid splendour which burns like gold and bathes like blood. Along this fiery path and valley, the tossing waves by which the swell of the sea is restlessly divided, lift themselves in dark, indefinite, fantastic forms, each casting a faint and ghastly shadow behind it along the illumined foam. They do not rise everywhere, but three or four together in wild groups, fitfully and furiously, as the under strength of the swell compels or permits them ; leaving between them treacherous space of level and whirling water, now lighted with green and lamp-like fire, now flashing back the gold of the declining sun, now fearfully dyed from above with the indistinguishable images of the burning clouds, which fall upon them in flakes of crimson and scarlet, and give to the reckless waves the added motion of their own fiery flying."-–*Modern Painters*, vol. i.

*   *   *   *   *

"The white surges rose bodily and slowly, as with some awful deliberation, up the rock on which the light-house stands, and along the high rock-married structure, swallowing the whole solid mass, more than a hundred feet of granite, shrouding it from sight, the phantom armour of white water (not spray, solid water !) meeting above the lanthorn in a pointed flame, and redescending. You should climb to the very extreme point, and stand on a ledge of granite, if the direction of the wind permit the water to be carried somewhat away,—then will you behold solid moving mountains of dark bulk, of uncertain wavering ridge, following one another, their emerald crests smoking, heavily arching over in loud ruin upon where shadow grows in hollows under their altitudes impending ! What Niagaras, and Mosioa-tunyas, thundering upwards against sable island fortresses will you witness !—all under low drifting storm-rack, in a dun rush of blown rain, wind, and ocean confounding their tremendous sound together. But under these raging waves, they say, lies the fair land of Lyonesse, where fell King Arthur when—

> "'All day long the noise of battle rolled
>   Among the mountains by the winter sea.'

"In one place there is a tract of pale sand left in the midst of the sea at low tide around which the water, emerald green in sunlight, paler beryl in misty weather, slowly sweeps. Through the mist one dimly discerns vast languid wreaths of spent foam, floating 'many a rood' on the leaden wilderness."—"By Cornish Seas" (*From Essays on Poetry and Poets*).

The Editor is indebted to Mr. Theodore Watts (whose "Ode to Mother Carey's Chicken," given in this volume, shows that he has a peculiar right to speak upon sea-poetry) for permission to quote the following suggestive passages from his essay upon "Poets and the Sea"—passages so particularly appropriate that they might have been written as a preface to some such compilation as "Sea-Music" :—

"From time immemorial the poets have taxed their energies to render in words the beauty of the earth; and so infinite in variety is that beauty, so ever growing, and so ever changing, that the latest picture by the latest poet seems

if he have the true eye for nature, as fresh and
unworn as the descriptions of Homer. But this
is not so with the sea. After a few epithets
the poet can say nothing to recall the beauty
of her whose deepest and most abiding charm
is oneness — monotony of voice, and even
monotony of colour, save for such reflected
hues as she can steal from the riches of
heaven. The truth, of course, is that while
the sea seems to be alive, but is really a mere
waste of dead matter tossed about uncon
sciously by the winds, the earth, though without motion, contains within her warm bosom,
not only a nursery for life, but very life itself.
This is why it is so easy for the literary artist to
paint the earth, so difficult for him to paint the
sea. With very few exceptions the poets do
not attempt to do it, but instead depict the
sensations and emotions to which the sea gives
birth in its impact on the body and the soul of
man.

"Perhaps to enjoy to the full all the delights
the sea has in store for us there is needed something more than the capacity for being exhilarated
by the buffets of the wind and the tossing of
billows. It may even be said, perhaps, that he who
would enjoy the fierce delights of a storm at sea

more than most others is precisely he who might not have the fullest appreciation of the sea's permanent message—the message of resignation to the awards of Fate, recognition of the wild and wonderful romance of the human poem, and sweet acceptance of Death, the soother of sorrows—precisely he who might feel most sorely that ' monotony ' which the larger portion of good sailors are apt to complain of, though in this very monotony lies the sea's greatest fascination for certain temperaments. There is many a man who can get a rapture of enjoyment from a short trip in a yacht, or even from a rapid steam-run across the Atlantic, who would find a long voyage with a handful of prosaic companions positively insupportable.

" In these days it cannot be too frequently iterated and reiterated that to the sea England and the English-speaking race owe everything. Whatever may be said of England's decadence as a physical force among the other great physical forces of Europe, her unique destiny as the great moral force of the world is becoming more and more obvious every day. The peculiar racial characteristics of her people, her language, her literature, her traditions, are colouring the great tide of human life, as the mighty river beyond the peaks of Káf coloured, according to the Mohammedan fancy, the waters of the ocean 'as with the living blood of all gems.'

"And what is the cause of this? The feverish attention lately given to colonial matters on the Continent, and the talk of Imperial Federation in England, show what is the general opinion as to the cause. A great racial struggle for life is imminent in Europe, outlets for the teeming populations of the old world are urgently demanded, and practically there are no new countries left to develope. In the new world of the North-West and in the new world scattered over the boundless bosom of the great Southern Ocean the whole of the lands in the temperate zones have been appropriated, and by whom? Mainly by the English. That this is the cause of England's present dominance and of her stupendous future has now become an axiom on the Continent.

"But what is the cause of the cause? How has it come about that in the unfilled lands of the temperate zone—in North America, in Africa, in Australia—almost every square mile of land is in the hands of Englishmen? Among Englishmen we, of course, include our brothers of the United States, with whom we of this island share with pride our blood and traditions, and between whom and us the bonds of affectionate sympathy are becoming closer and closer every year and every day. Is it true, as English chauvinists assume it to be, that in the great racial struggle for life the Englishman is specially organized for success? Does the English race really exhibit any superiority over the other European races? Are Englishmen and Americans more courageous than Germans or more energetic? Are they more high-spirited than the French, or more deft, or more frugal? Are they more nobly endowed than the Italians with that dignified common sense which is said to be the very salt of life? To answer these questions in the affirmative would, no doubt, be pleasant, but would it be justified by the facts? Would any English employer of labour, skilled or unskilled, answer them in the affirmative? No: there is another cause—a cause wholly unrelated to race—for the prospects of the English race. That cause is the sea.

"From no peculiar merit of its own, but from the favouritism of circumstance is the English race destined to hold the world in its hand. The Englishman's birth-place having been the only large and fruitful island of the Old World, he has become the child of the sea. That the high road of the ocean should lead him all over the world was simply inevitable. Hence England's destiny as "the august mother of empires" should give rise to no vainglory in any Englishman's breast; but rather it should give rise to a feeling of modesty, almost of humiliation, before responsibilities so vast. It should cause us to ask ourselves, Are we really and fully worthy of this favouritism of the sea? Thanks to the 'silver streak,' which is worth an entire European army, the English race, instead of exhausting its force, as the other less lucky races have been obliged to do, in defending frontiers, has been enabled to give all its energies to strengthening its limbs at home and finding fresh fields in which to exercise them abroad.

It is, however, only of late years that the fact has been ignored that England owes her very existence to the sea—that without the sea she is nothing. The finest marine lyric in this or any other language, 'Ye Mariners of England,' was written, as the greatest contemporary nautical writer has pointed out, by a man who had no knowledge whatever of the sailor's calling. And there is no need whatever, as Mr. Clark Russell goes on to say, why the ' So ho's,' ' Heave-ho's,' and ' Pull away, boys,' of the Dibdin school of marine poets should be revived. So the landsman, if he have the true sea-feeling, need not shrink from entering the field. Thus considered, a writer of good sea-poetry would confer a service on the country should he revive in the breasts of Englishmen the old passion for the traditions of the English navy."

It is curious to note that even as the finest marine lyric in our language was written by one who was no seaman, so perhaps the most striking marine sonnet in our language is the production of a writer who was certainly not in the general sense a poet of nature, whose observation of nature, indeed, was almost solely the outcome of the pictorial instinct. Rossetti undoubtedly saw not only truly but acutely ; but it was the artist noting " effects," not the poet perceiving subtle beauties. The sonnet in question was written on the occasion of the meeting at an anniversary banquet of the three remaining veterans who as lads had served under Nelson at his greatest sea-fight, and was appropriately entitled by Rossetti " The Last Three from Trafalgar."

The Last Three from Trafalgar.

In grappled ships around The Victory,
    Three boys did England's Duty with stout cheer,
    While one dread truth was kept from every ear,
More dire than deafening fire that churned the sea :
For in the flag-ship's weltering cockpit, he
    Who was the Battle's Heart without a peer,
    He who had seen all fearful sights save Fear,
Was passing from all life save Victory.

And round the old memorial board to-day,
    Three greybeards—each a war-worn British Tar—
    View through the mist of years that hour afar :
Who soon shall greet, 'mid memories of fierce fray,
The impassioned soul which on its radiant way
    Soared through the fiery cloud of Trafalgar.

The Editor desires the present writer to express her indebtedness to all the living writers who are represented in this volume of Sea-Music. Without such collaboration this book could not have been compiled—for the reason already stated, that most of our sea-poetry has been written by Victorian poets. The compilation was commenced some three or four years ago, and was in great part accomplished by the beginning of 1886. Ill-health and other unavoidable causes have prevented its earlier publication. The delay is certainly not to be

regretted, as the Editor has been able to include many strains of sea-music, without which
this anthology would lose much of what most
readers will probably find to be its present
charm.   Much herein to be found will already
be familiar to all lovers of English poetry.

If this volume of "scents and murmurs from
the infinite Sea," prove a source of refreshment
and delight to some, of stimulus to others—if,
in howsoever slight measure, it help to quicken
or keep alive that sea-love and sea-pride which
are our national heritage, the Editor will be
grateful indeed that she undertook what has
for so long been a delightful labour.

SEA-MUSIC.

FROM " PARADISE LOST."

Over all the face of Earth
Main ocean flowed, not idle, but, with warm
Prolific humour softening all her globe,
Fermented the great mother to conceive,
Satiate with genial moisture ; when God said,
" Be gathered now, ye waters under heaven,
Into one place, and let dry land appear ! "
Immediately the mountains huge appear
Emergent, and their broad bare backs upheave
Into the clouds ; their tops ascend the sky.
So high as heaved the tumid hills, so low
Down sunk a hollow bottom broad and deep,
Capacious bed of waters.   Thither they
Hasted with glad precipitance, uprolled,
As drops on dust conglobing, from the dry :
Part rise in crystal wall, or ridge direct,
For haste ; such flight the great command impressed
On the swift floods.   As armies at the call
Of trumpet (for of armies thou hast heard)
Troop to the standard, so the watery throng,

B

Wave rolling after wave, where way they found—
If steep, with torrent rapture, if through plain,
Soft-ebbing ; nor withstood them rock or hill ;
But they, or underground, or circuit wide
With serpent error wandering, found their way,
And on the washy ooze deep channels wore :
Easy ere God had bid the ground be dry,
All but within those banks where rivers now
Stream, and perpetual draw their humid train.
The dry land Earth, and the great receptacle
Of congregated waters He called Seas.

MILTON.

FROM "OTHELLO."

METHINKS the wind has spoke aloud at land ;
A fuller blast ne'er shook our battlements :
If it hath ruffian'd so upon the sea
What ribs of oak, when mountains melt upon them,
Can hold the mortise? . . .
For do but stand upon the foaming shore,
The chidden billow seems to pelt the clouds ;
The wind-shaked surge, with high and monstrous mane,
Seems to cast water on the burning bear,
And quench the guards of the ever-fixed pole :
I never did such molestation view
On the enchafèd flood.

SHAKESPEARE.

(*Enter* ARIEL, *invisible, playing and singing,*
FERDINAND *following.*)

ARIEL *sings.*

COME unto these yellow sands,
    And then take hands :
Courtsied when you have and kiss'd
    The wild waves whist,
Foot it featly here and there.

*   *   *   *   *

Fer. Where should this music be ? i' the air or the
        earth ?
It sounds no more : and, sure, it waits upon
Some god o' the island.   Sitting on a bank,
Weeping again the king my father's wreck,
This music crept by me upon the waters,
Allaying both their fury and my passion
With its sweet air : thence I have follow'd it,
Or it hath drawn me rather.   But 'tis gone.
No, it begins again.

ARIEL *sings.*

Full fathom five thy father lies ;
    Of his bones are coral made ;
Those are pearls that were his eyes :
    Nothing of him that doth fade
But doth suffer a sea change
Into something rich and strange.
Sea-nymphs hourly ring his knell.

SHAKESPEARE.

FROM "CYMBELINE."

             REMEMBER, sir, my liege,
The kings your ancestors, together with
The natural bravery of your isle, which stands
As Neptune's park, ribbed and paled in
With rocks unscaleable and roaring waters
With sands that will not bear your enemies' boats
But sucks them up to topmast.

SHAKESPEARE.

FROM "THE INVOCATION TO SLEEP."

KING HENRY IV. PART II.

WILT thou upon the high and giddy mast
Seal up the ship-boy's eyes, and rock his brains
In cradle of the rude imperious surge ;
And in the visitation of the winds,
Who take the ruffian billows by the top,
Curling their monstrous heads and hanging them
With deafening clamour in the slippery clouds,
That, with the hurly, death itself awakes ?

SHAKESPEARE.

LIKE as the waves make towards the pebbled shore
So do our minutes hasten to their end.

SHAKESPEARE.

FROM " KING RICHARD III."

METHOUGHT I saw a thousand fearful wrecks ;
A thousand men that fishes gnaw'd upon ;
Wedges of gold, great anchors, heaps of pearl,
Inestimable stones, unvalued jewels,
All scatter'd in the bottom of the sea.
Some lay in dead men's skulls ; and in those holes
Where eyes did once inhabit, there were crept,
As 'twere in scorn of eyes, reflecting gems,
That woo'd the slimy bottom of the deep,
And mock'd the dead bones that lay scatter'd by.

SHAKESPEARE.

FROM " HENRY VI."

NOW sways it this way, like a mighty sea
Forc'd by the tide to combat with the wind ;
Now sways it that way, like the self-same sea
Forc'd to retire by fury of the wind :
Sometime the flood prevails ; and then the wind :
Now one the better ; then another best ;
Both tugging to be victors, breast to breast,
Yet neither conqueror nor conquered.

SHAKESPEARE.

THE rough seas, that spare not any man.

SHAKESPEARE.

THE deep-mouth'd sea.

SHAKESPEARE.

FROM "THE BEACON."

No fish stir in our heaving net,
And the sky is dark and the night is wet ;
And we must ply the lusty oar,
For the tide is ebbing from the shore ;
And sad are they whose faggots burn,
So kindly stored for our return.

Our boat is small and the tempest raves,
And naught is heard but the lashing waves,
And the sullen roar of the angry sea,
And the wild winds piping drearily ;
Yet sea and tempest rise in vain,
We'll bless our blazing hearths again.

Push bravely, mates !   Our guiding star
Now from its towerlet streameth far,
And now along the nearing strand,
See, swiftly moves yon flaming brand :
Before the midnight watch be past
We'll quaff our bowl and mock the blast.

JOANNA BAILLIE.

A HYMN OF THE SEA.

THE sea is mighty, but a mightier sways
His restless billows.   Thou, whose hands have scooped
His boundless gulfs and built his shore, thy breath,
That moved in the beginning o'er his face
Moves o'er it evermore.   The obedient waves
To its strong motion roll, and rise and fall.
Still from that realm of rain thy cloud goes up,
As at the first, to water the great earth,
And keep her valleys green.   A hundred realms
Watch its broad shadow warping on the wind,
And in the drooping shower, with gladness hear
Thy promise of the harvest.   I look forth
Over the boundless blue, where joyously
The bright crests of innumerable waves
Glance to the sun at once, as when the hands
Of a great multitude are upward flung
In acclamation.   I behold the ships
Gliding from cape to cape, from isle to isle,
Or stemming towards far lands, or hastening home
From the Old World.   It is thy friendly breeze
That bears them, with the riches of the land,
And treasure of dear lives, till, in the port,
The shouting seamen climb and furl the sail.

But who shall bide thy tempest, who shall face
The blast that wakes the fury of the sea ?

O God ! thy justice makes the world turn pale,
When on the armèd fleet, that royally
Bears down the surges, carrying war, to smite
Some city, or invade some thoughtless realm,
Descends the fierce tornado.   The vast hulks
Are whirled like chaff upon the waves ; the sails
Fly, rent like webs of gossamer ; the masts
Are snapped asunder ; downward from the decks,
Downward are slung, into the fathomless gulf
Their cruel engines, and their hosts, arrayed
In trappings of the battlefield, are whelmed
By whirlpools, or dashed dead upon the rocks.
Then stand the nations still with awe, and pause,
A moment, from the bloody work of war.

    These restless surges eat away the shores
Of earth's old continents ; the fertile plain
Welters in shallows, headlands crumble down,
And the tide drifts the sea-sand in the streets
Of the drowned city.   Thou, meanwhile, afar
In the green chambers of the middle sea,
Where broadest spread the waters and the line
Sinks deepest, while no eye beholds thy work,
Creator ! thou dost teach the coral-worm
To lay his mighty reefs.   From age to age
He builds beneath the waters, till, at last,
His bulwarks overtop the brine, and check
The long wave rolling from the southern pole
To break upon Japan.   Thou bidd'st the fires,
That smoulder under ocean, heave on high
The new-made mountains, and uplift their peaks,
A place of refuge for the storm-driven bird.

The birds and wafting billows plant the rifts
With herb and tree ; sweet fountains gush ; sweet airs
Ripple the living lakes that, fringed with flowers,
Are gathered in the hollows.　Thou dost look
On thy creation and pronounce it good.
Its valleys, glorious in their summer green,
Praise thee in silent beauty, and its woods,
Swept by the murmuring winds of ocean, join
The murmuring shores in a perpetual hymn

WILLIAM CULLEN BRYANT

AN under-current, strong to draw
Million of waves into itself, and run,
From sea to sea, impervious to the sun
And ploughing storm.

WORDSWORTH.

THE world so hushed !
The stilly murmur of the distant sea
Tells us of silence.

COLERIDGE

APOSTROPHE TO THE OCEAN.

THERE is a pleasure in the pathless woods,
There is a rapture on the lonely shore,
There is society, where none intrudes,
 By the deep Sea, and music in its roar :
I love not man the less, but Nature more,
From these our interviews, in which I steal
From all I may be, or have been before,
To mingle with the Universe, and feel
What I can ne'er express, yet cannot all conceal.

Roll on, thou deep and dark blue Ocean—roll !
Ten thousand fleets sweep over thee in vain ;
Man marks the earth with ruin—his control
Stops with the shore ;—upon the watery plain
The wrecks are all thy deed, nor doth remain
A shadow of man's ravage, save his own,
When, for a moment, like a drop of rain,
He sinks into thy depths with bubbling groan,
Without a grave, unknell'd, uncoffin'd, and unknown.

His steps are not upon thy paths,—thy fields
Are not a spoil for him,—thou dost arise
And shake him from thee ; the vile strength he wields
For earth's destruction thou dost all despise,
Spurning him from thy bosom to the skies,
And send'st him, shivering in thy playful spray,
And howling, to his gods, where haply lies

His petty hope in some near port or bay,
And dashest him again to earth :—there let him lay.

The armaments which thunderstrike the walls
Of rock-built cities, bidding nations quake,
And monarchs tremble in their capitals,
The oak leviathans, whose huge ribs make
Their clay creator the vain title take
Of lord of thee, and arbiter of war ;
These are thy toys, and, as the snowy flake,
They melt into thy yeast of waves, which mar
Alike the Armada's pride, or spoils of Trafalgar.

Thy shores are empires, changed in all save thee—
Assyria, Greece, Rome, Carthage, what are they?
Thy waters wasted them while they were free,
And many a tyrant since : their shores obey
The stranger, slave, or savage ; their decay
Has dried up realms to deserts : not so thou,
Unchangeable save to thy wild waves' play—
Time writes no wrinkle on thine azure brow—
Such as creation's dawn beheld, thou rollest now.

Thou glorious mirror, where the Almighty's form
Glasses itself in tempests ; in all time,
Calm, or convulsed—in breeze, or gale, or storm,
Icing the pole, or in the torrid clime
Dark-heaving ; boundless, endless, and sublime—
The image of Eternity—the throne
Of the Invisible ; even from out thy slime

The monsters of the deep are made ; each zone
Obeys thee ; thou goest forth, dread, fathomless, alone.

And I have loved thee, Ocean ! and my joy
Of youthful sports was on thy breast to be
Borne like thy bubbles, onward : from a boy
I wanton'd with thy breakers—they to me
Were a delight ; and if the freshening sea
Made them a terror—'twas a pleasing fear,
For I was as it were a child of thee,
And trusted to thy billows far and near,
And laid my hand upon thy mane—as I do here.

BYRON.

ONCE more upon the waters ! yet once more !
And the waves bound beneath me as a steed
That knows his rider.   Welcome to their roar !
Swift be their guidance, wheresoe'er it lead !
Though the strain'd mast should quiver as a reed,
And the rent canvas fluttering strew the gale,
Still must I on : for I am as a weed,
Flung from the rock, on Ocean's foam, to sail
Where'er the surge may sweep, the tempest's breath
    prevail.

BYRON.

As the spring-tides, with heavy splash,
From the cliffs invading dash
Huge fragments, sapp'd by the ceaseless flow,
Till white and thundering down they go,
Like the avalanche's snow
On the Alpine vales below.

BYRON.

Now overhead a rainbow, bursting through
  The scattering clouds, shone, spanning the dark sea,
Resting its bright base on the quivering blue,
  And all within its arch appear'd to be
Clearer than that without, and its wide hue
  Wax'd broad and waving like a banner free,
Then changed like to a bow that's bent, and then
Forsook the dim eyes of these shipwrecked men.

BYRON.

It was a wild and weather-beaten coast,
  With cliffs above, and a broad sandy shore,
Guarded by shoals and rocks as by a host,
  With here and there a creek, whose aspect wore
A better welcome to the tempest-tost ;
  And rarely ceas'd the haughty billow's roar,
Save on the dead long summer days, which make
The outstretch'd ocean glitter like a lake.

BYRON.

The coast—I think it was the coast that I
  Was just describing—Yes, it *was* the coast—
Lay at this period quiet as the sky,
  The sands untumbled, the blue waves untost,
And all was stillness, save the sea-bird's cry,
  And dolphin's leap, and little billow crost
By some low rock or shelve, that made it fret
Against the boundary it scarcely wet.

BYRON.

THE MARINERS OF ENGLAND.

YE Mariners of England !
That guard our native seas ;
Whose flag has braved a thousand years,
The battle and the breeze !
Your glorious standard launch again
To match another foe !
And sweep through the deep,
While the stormy tempests blow ;
While the battle rages loud and long,
And the stormy winds do blow !

The spirits of your fathers
Shall start from every wave !—
For the deck it was their field of fame,
And Ocean was their grave :
Where Blake and mighty Nelson fell,
Your manly hearts shall glow,
As ye sweep through the deep,
While the stormy winds do blow ;
While the battle rages loud and long,
And the stormy winds do blow !

Britannia needs no bulwarks,
No towers along the steep ;
Her march is o'er the mountain-waves,
Her home is on the deep ;
With thunders from her native oak,

She quells the floods below,—
As they roar on the shore,
When the stormy winds do blow ;
When the battle rages loud and long,
And the stormy winds do blow !

The meteor-flag of England
Shall yet terrific burn ;
Till danger's troubled night depart,
And the star of peace return.
Then, then, ye ocean warriors !
Our song and feast shall flow
To the fame of your name,
When the storm has ceased to blow ;
When the fiery fight is heard no more,
And the storm has ceased to blow.

CAMPBELL.

       MIGHTY Sea !
Cameleon-like thou changest, but there's love
In all thy change, and constant sympathy
With yonder Sky—thy mistress ; from her brow
Thou tak'st thy moods and wear'st her colours on
Thy faithful bosom ; morning's milky white,
Noon's sapphire, or the saffron glow of eve ;
And all thy balmier hours, fair Element,
Have such divine complexion—crisped smiles,
Luxuriant heavings, and sweet whisperings,
That little is the wonder Love's own Queen
From thee of old was fabled to have sprung—
Creation's common ! which no human power
Can parcel or inclose ; the lordliest floods
And cataracts that the tiny hands of man
Can tame, conduct, or bound, are drops of dew
To thee that could'st subdue the Earth itself,
And brook'st commandment from the heavens alone
For marshalling thy waves.
         CAMPBELL.

  'TIS said, fantastic ocean doth enfold
  The likeness of whate'er on land is seen.

         WORDSWORTH.

  THE vast salt eternal deep.

         BYRON.

OLD Ocean was
Infinity of ages ere we breathed
Existence—and he will be beautiful
When all the living world that sees him now
Shall roll unconscious dust around the sun.
Quelling from age to age the vital throb
In human hearts, Death shall not subjugate
The pulse that dwells in his stupendous breast,
Or interdict his minstrelsy to sound
In thundering concert with the quiring winds ;
But long as Man to parent Nature owns
Instinctive homage, and in times beyond
The power of thought to reach, bard after bard
Shall sing thy glory, beatific Sea.

CAMPBELL.

THE ghost of day yet haunts the troubled west,
A shiver creeps along the pallid seas.

WILLIAM FALCONER.

AND small are the white-crested that play near,
And smaller onward are the purple waves.

W. S. LANDOR.

THIS Sea that bares her bosom to the Moon.

WORDSWORTH.

C

           PLEASANT Sea !
.   .   .   Earth has not a plain
So boundless or so beautiful as thine ;
The eagle's vision cannot take it in :
The lightning's wing, too weak to sweep its space,
Sinks half-way o'er it like a wearied bird :
It is the mirror of the stars, where all
Their hosts within the concave firmament,
Gay marching to the music of the spheres,
Can see themselves at once.

                       CAMPBELL.

THE tirèd ocean crawls along the beach
Sobbing a wordless sorrow to the moon.

                   WILLIAM FALCONER.

LAUGHED on their shores the hoarse seas ; the yearning
     ocean swelled upward.

                     COLERIDGE.

A STORM of waves break foaming on the strand.

                     COLERIDGE.

FROM "THE ANCIENT MARINER."

THE fair breeze blew, the white foam flew,
  The furrow follow'd free ;
We were the first that ever burst
  Into that silent sea.

Down dropt the breeze, the sails dropt down,
  'Twas sad as sad could be ;
And we did speak only to break
  The silence of the sea ;

All in a hot and copper sky,
  The bloody Sun, at noon,
Right up above the mast did stand,
  No bigger than the moon.

Day after day, day after day
  We stuck, nor breath nor motion ;
As idle as a painted ship
  Upon a painted ocean.

Water, water, everywhere,
  And all the boards did shrink ;
Water, water, everywhere,
  And not a drop to drink.

The very deep did rot : O Christ !
  That ever this should be !

Yea, slimy things did crawl with legs
  Upon a slimy sea.

About, about, in reel and rout
  The death-fires danced at night ;
The water, like a witch's oils,
  Burnt green, and blue, and white.

*   *   *   *

The moving moon went up the sky,
  And nowhere did abide ;
Softly she was going up,
  And a star or two beside.

Her beams bemocked the sultry main,
  Like April hoar-frost spread ;
But where the ship's huge shadow lay,
The charmèd water burnt alway
  A still and awful red.

Beyond the shadow of the ship
  I watched the water-snakes ;
They moved in tracks of shining white,
And when they reared, the elfish light
  Fell off in hoary flakes.

Within the shadow of the ship
  I watched their rich attire ;
Blue, glossy green, and velvet black,
They coiled and swam ; and every track
  Was a flash of golden fire.

COLERIDGE.

A WET SHEET AND A FLOWING SEA.

A WET sheet and a flowing sea,
  A wind that follows fast,
And fills the white and rustling sail,
  And bends the gallant mast ;
And bends the gallant mast, my boys,
  While, like the eagle free,
Away the good ship flies, and leaves
  Old England on the lee.

O for a soft and gentle wind !
  I heard a fair one cry ;
But give to me the snoring breeze,
  And white waves heaving high ;
And white waves heaving high, my boys,
  The good ship tight and free—
The world of waters is our home,
  And merry men are we.

There's tempest in yon horned moon,
  And lightning in yon cloud ;
And hark, the music, mariners,
  The wind is piping loud ;
The wind is piping loud, my boys,
  The lightning flashes free—
While the hollow oak our palace is,
  Our heritage the sea.

ALLAN CUNNINGHAM.

ATLANTIC COAST SCENERY.

THE CLIFFS.

These iron-rifted cliffs, that o'er the deep,
  Wave-worn and thunder-scarred, enormous lower,
  Stand like the work of some primeval Power,
Titan or Demiurgos, that would keep
Firm ward for ever o'er the bastioned steep
  Of turret-crowned Beltard, or mightiest Moher:
  Vainly beneath, as though they would devour
The rooted rocks before them, reel and leap
The headlong waves: and as a plumed phalanx,
  Crushed in the assault of some strong citadel,
Indomitable still, its shattered ranks
    Cheers to the breach again, and yet again,
  So from the battling billows bursts the swell
    Of a more awful combat than of men!

Sir Aubrey De Vere.

COAST SCENERY.

THE SOLITUDES OF MALBAY.

AND O ! ye solitudes of rocks and waters,
   And medicinable gales and sounds Lethean,
Remote from strife and fratricidal slaughters,
   Have I not sighed to hear your mighty Pæan,
   Reverberating through the Empyrean !
And yearned to gaze while your white-throated surges
   Leap, and dissolve in air, like shapes Protean,
That sport in the sunset, as the moon emerges
Over the sea-cliff?　Have I not felt the longing
   Then most intensely, when the storm-steed rushes
O'er the wild waves tumultuously thronging,
   Smiting their wan crests,—scattering as he crushes ;—
To stand on some lone peak, and hear, from under
Its caverned base, the ocean's melancholy thunder ?

SIR AUBREY DE VERE.

COAST SCENERY.

SPANISH POINT.

THE waters—O the waters !—Wild and glooming,
　Beneath the stormy pall that shrouds the sky,
On, through the deepening mist more darkly looming
　Plumed with the pallid foam funereally,
Onward, like death, they come, the rocks entombing !
　Nor thunder knell is needful from on high ;
Nor sound of signal gun, momently booming
　O'er the disastrous deep ; nor seaman's cry !
And yet,—if aught were wanting—manifold
　Mementoes haunt those reefs : how proud that Host
Of Spain and Rome so smitten were of old,
　By God's decree, along this fatal coast,
And over all their purple and their gold,
Mitre, and helm, and harp, the avenging waters rolled !

SIR AUBREY DE VERE.

COAST SCENERY.

MALBAY SANDS.

IT may not be, because this tranquil hour,
  Brightening elsewhere to beauty scenes more grand,
  Here lights with milder beam a lowlier strand,
And that yon sea, like a tired warrior,
For quiet joy hath laid aside his power,
  That unattractive, therefore, must expand
  This graceful curvature of golden sand
By the ebbing tide left shining.   Vernal bower
Is scarce more fragrant than those weeds marine
  Fringing the chrysolite, pellucid, wells,
  Wave-worn in the rock, where children stoop for shells,
And braiding yon gray reef with tresses green,
  Where sunset loiterers love at eve to stand—
  Dark groups, with shadows lengthening to the land.

SIR AUBREY DE VERE.

THE SEA CAVE.

HARDLY we breathe, although the air be free :
    How massively doth awful Nature pile
    The living rock like some cathedral aisle,
Sacred to silence and the solemn sea.
How that clear pool lies sleeping tranquilly,
    And under its glassed surface seems to smile,
    With many hues, a mimic grove the while
Of foliage submarine—shrub, flower, and tree.

Beautiful scene, and fitted to allure
    The printless footsteps of some sea-born maid,
    Who here, with her green tresses disarrayed,
'Mid the clear bath, unfearing and secure,
    May sport at noontide in the caverned shade,
Cold as the shadow, as the waters pure.

THOMAS DOUBLEDAY.

DISTANT SOUND OF THE SEA AT EVENING

YET, rolling far up some green mountain-dale,
Oft let me hear, as ofttimes I have heard,
Thy swell, thou deep ! when evening calls the bird
And bee to rest ; when summer tints grow pale,
Seen through the gathering of a dewy veil ;
And peasant-steps are hastening to repose,
And gleaming flocks lie down, and flower-cups close
To the last whisper of the falling gale.
Then, midst the dying of all other sound,
When the Soul hears thy distant voice profound,
Lone-worshipping, and knows that through the
'Twill worship still, then most its anthem-tone
Speaks to our being of the Eternal One,
Who girds tired nature with unslumbering night

FELICIA D. HEMANS.

THE TREASURES OF THE DEEP.

WHAT hidest thou in thy treasure-caves and cells,
  Thou hollow-sounding and mysterious main?
Pale glistening pearls, and rainbow-coloured shells,
  Bright things which gleam unrecked of and in vain!—
Keep, keep thy riches, melancholy sea!
    We ask not such from thee.

Yet more, the depths have more!—What wealth untold,
  Far down, and shining through their stillness lies!
Thou hast the starry gems, the burning gold,
  Won from ten thousand royal argosies!—
Sweep o'er thy spoils, thou wild and wrathful main!
    Earth claims not *these* again!

Yet more! the depths have more! Thy waves have rolled
  Above the cities of a world gone by!
Sand hath filled up the palaces of old,
  Sea-weed o'ergrown the halls of revelry—
Dash o'er them, ocean! in thy scornful play!
    Man yields them to decay!

Yet more! the billows and the depths have more!
  High hearts and brave are gathered to thy breast!
They hear not now the booming waters roar,
  The battle-thunders will not break their rest—
Keep thy red gold and gems, thou stormy grave!
    Give back the true and brave.

Give back the lost and lovely !—those for whom
  The place was kept at board and hearth so long !
The prayer went up, through midnight's breathless
    gloom,
  And the vain yearning woke 'midst festal song !
Hold fast thy buried isles, thy towers o'erthrown—
    But all is not thine own !

To thee the love of women hath gone down,
  Dark flow thy tides o'er manhood's noble head,
O'er youth's bright locks, and beauty's flowery crown !
  Yet must thou hear a voice—Restore the dead !
Earth shall reclaim her precious things from thee !—
    Restore the dead, thou Sea !

Felicia D. Hemans.

And light and sound ebbed from the earth,
Like the tide of the full and weary sea
To the depths of its own tranquillity.

Shelley.

                    The motion
Of waves, the breezes fragrant from the sea,
And cry of birds, combine one glorious symphony.

Sir Aubrey De Vere.

THE LOST EXPEDITION.

Lift—lift, ye mists, from off the silent coast,
　Folded in endless winter's chill embraces ;
Unshroud for us awhile our brave ones lost !
　　Let us behold their faces !

In vain—the North hath hid them from our sight ;
　The snow their winding-sheet,—their only dirges
The groan of icebergs in the polar night,
　　Racked by the savage surges.

No funeral torches with a smoky glare
　Shone a farewell upon their shrouded faces ;—
No monumental pillar tall and fair
　　Towers o'er their resting-places.

But Northern streamers flare the long night through
　Over the cliffs stupendous, fraught with peril,
Of icebergs tinted with a ghostly hue
　　Of amethyst and beryl.

No human tears upon their graves are shed—
　Tears of domestic love, or pity holy ;
But snowflakes from the gloomy sky o'erhead,
　　Down shuddering, settle slowly.

Yet history shrines them with her mighty dead,
　The hero-seamen of this isle of Britain,

And, when the brighter scroll of heaven is read,
   There will their names be written.

                         THOMAS HOOD.

Now lay thine ear against this golden sand,
And thou shalt hear the music of the sea,
Those hollow tunes it plays against the land,—
Is 't not a rich and wondrous melody?
I have lain hours, and fancied in its tone
I heard the languages of ages gone.

                         THOMAS HOOD.

          THE sea-breeze moans
Thro' yon reft house !   O'er rolling stones
       In bold ambitious sweep
The onward-surging tides supply
The silence of the cloudless sky
       With mimic thunders deep.

                         COLERIDGE.

WHY stand we gazing on the sparkling Brine,
With wonder smit by its transparency,
And all enraptured with its purity?—
Because the unstained, the pure, the crystalline,
Have ever in them something of benign.

                         WORDSWORTH.

TO AILSA ROCK.

HEARKEN, thou craggy ocean pyramid !
 Give answer from thy voice, the sea-fowl's screams !
 When were thy shoulders mantled in huge streams ?
When, from the sun, was thy broad forehead hid?
How long is 't since the mighty power bid
 Thee heave to airy sleep from fathom dreams?
 Sleep in the lap of thunder or sun-beams,
Or when grey clouds are thy cold cover-lid?
Thou answer'st not, for thou art dead asleep !
 Thy life is but two dead eternities—
The last in air, the former in the deep ;
 First with the whales, last with the eagle-skies—
Drown'd wast thou till an earthquake made thee steep,
 Another cannot wake thy giant size.

KEATS.

FROM " EPISTLE TO MY BROTHER GEORGE."

THE freshest breeze I caught.
E'en now, I am pillow'd on a bed of flowers
That crowns a lofty cliff, which proudly towers
Above the ocean waves.　The stalks, and blades,
Chequer my tablet with their quivering shades.
On one side is a field of drooping oats,
Through which the poppies show their scarlet coats,
So pert and useless, that they bring to mind
The scarlet coats that pester human-kind
And on the other side, outspread, is seen
Ocean's blue mantle, streak'd with purple and green ;
Now 'tis I see a canvass'd ship, and now
Mark the bright silver curling round her prow.
I see the lark down-dropping to his nest,
And the broad-wing'd sea-gull never at rest ;
For when no more he spreads his feathers free,
His breast is dancing on the restless sea.

KEATS.

THE Ocean with its vastness, its blue green,
　Its ships, its rocks, its caves, its hopes, its fears, —
　Its voice mysterious, which whoso hears
Must think on what will be, and what has been.

KEATS.

THE surgy murmurs of the lonely sea.

KEATS.

D

FROM " ENDYMION."

WIDE sea, that one continuous murmur breeds
Along the pebbled shore of memory !

*   *   *   *   *

Enforced, at the last by ocean's foam
I found me ; by my fresh, my native home,
Its tempering coolness, to my life akin,
Came salutary as I waded in :
And, with a blind voluptuous rage, I gave
Battle to the swollen billow-ridge, and drave
Large froth before me, while there yet remain'd
Hale strength, nor from my bones all marrow drain'd
                                        KEATS.

THE moving waters at their priest-like task
Of pure ablution round earth's human shores.

                                        KEATS.

        MAGIC casements, opening on the foam
Of perilous seas, in faëry lands forlorn.
                                        KEATS.

THE rocks were silent, the wide sea did weave
An untumultuous fringe of silver foam,
Along the flat brown sands.
                                        KEATS.

A REFLECTION AT SEA.

SEE how, beneath the moonbeam's smile
   Yon little billow heaves its breast,
And foams and sparkles for awhile,
   Then murmuring subsides to rest.

Thus man, the sport of bliss and care,
   Rises on time's eventful sea ;
And, having swell'd a moment there,
   Thus melts into eternity.
THOMAS MOORE.

BUT I have sinuous shells of pearly hue
Within, and they that lustre have imbibed
In the sun's palace-porch, where when unyoked
His chariot-wheel stands midway in the wave :
Shake one and it awakens, then apply
Its polished lips to your attentive ear,
And it remembers its august abodes,
And murmurs as the ocean murmurs there.

W. S. LANDOR.

      GONE down the tide ;
And the long moonbeam on the hard wet sand
Lay like a jasper column half uprear'd.

W. S. LANDOR.

THE SEA—IN CALM.

LOOK what immortal floods the sunset pours
　　Upon us !—Mark how still (as though in dreams
　　Bound) the once wild and terrible Ocean seems !
How silent are the winds ! No billow roars,
But all is tranquil as Elysian shores !
　　The silver margin which aye runneth round
　　The moon-enchanted sea hath here no sound :
Even Echo speaks not on these radiant moors.
What ! is the giant of the ocean dead,
　　Whose strength was all unmatched beneath the sun !
　　No : he reposes.　Now his toils are done,
　　　More quiet than the babbling brooks is he.
So mightiest powers by deepest calms are fed,
　　And sleep, how oft, in things that gentlest be.

BRYAN WALLER PROCTER.

FROM "MARCIAN COLONNA."

O THOU vast Ocean !   Ever-sounding Sea !
Thou symbol of a drear immensity !
Thou thing that windest round the solid world
Like a huge animal, which, downward hurl'd
From the black clouds, lies weltering and alone,
Lashing and writhing till its strength be gone.
Thy voice is like the thunder, and thy sleep
Is as a giant's slumber, loud and deep.
Thou speakest in the East and in the West
At once, and on thy heavily-laden breast
Fleets come and go, and shapes that have no life
Or motion, yet are moved and meet in strife . . .
—Thou only, terrible Ocean, hast a power,
A will, a voice, and in thy wrathful hour,
When thou dost lift thine anger to the clouds,
A fearful and magnificent beauty shrouds
Thy broad green forehead.   If thy waves be driven
Backwards and forwards by the shifting wind,
How quickly dost thou thy great strength unbind,
And stretch thine arms, and war at once with Heaven

  Thou trackless and unmeasurable Main
On thee no record ever lived again
To meet the hand that writ it : line nor lead
Hath ever fathomed thy profoundest deeps,
Where haply the huge monster swells and steeps
King of his watery limit, who 'tis said,

Can move the mighty ocean into storm—
Oh ! wonderful thou art, great element :
And fearful in thy spleeny humours bent,
And lovely in repose ; thy summer form
Is beautiful, and when thy silver waves
Make music in earth's dark and winding caves,
I love to wander on thy pebbled beach,
Marking the sunlight at the evening hour,
And hearken to the thoughts thy waters teach—
" Eternity, Eternity, and Power."

BRYAN WALLER PROCTER.

THE glassy ocean hushed forgets to roar,
But trembling murmurs on the sandy shore ;
And lo ! his surface lovely to behold !
Glows in the west, a sea of living gold.

WILLIAM FALCONER.

THE stilly murmur of the distant sea
Tells us of silence.

COLERIDGE.

As 'mid the tuneful choir to keep
The diapason of the Deep.

SIR WALTER SCOTT.

FROM "THE STORMY PETREL."

A THOUSAND miles from land are we,
Tossing about on the roaring sea ;
From billow to bounding billow cast,
Like fleecy snow on the stormy blast :
The sails are scattered abroad like weeds ;
The strong masts shake, like quivering reeds ;
The hull, which all earthly strength disdains,
They strain, and they crack ; and hearts like stone
Their natural, hard, proud strength disown.

Up and down ! up and down !
From the base of the wave to the billow's crown
And amidst the flashing and feathery foam
The Stormy Petrel finds a home—
A home, if such a place may be,
For her who lives on the wide, wide sea,
On the craggy ice, in the frozen air,
And seeketh only her rocky lair
To warm her young, and to teach them spring
At once o'er the wave on their stormy wing !

BRYAN WALLER PROCTER.

FROM "THE LORD OF THE ISLES.'

THE helm, to his strong arm consign'd,
Gave the reef'd sail to meet the wind,
 And on her altered way,
Fierce bounding, forward sprung the ship,
Like greyhound starting from the slip
 To seize his flying prey.
Awaked before the rushing prow
The mimic fires of ocean glow,
 Those lightnings of the wave ;
Wild sparkles crest the broken tides
And, flashing round, the vessel's sides
 With elfish lustre lave.
While, far behind, their livid light
To the dark billows of the night
 A gloomy splendour gave,
It seems as if old Ocean shakes
From his dark brow the lucid flakes
 In envious pageantry,
To match the meteor-light that streaks
 Grim Hecla's midnight sky.

SIR WALTER SCOTT.

FROM "JULIAN AND MADDALO."

A BARE strand
Of hillocks, heaped from ever-shifting sand,
Matted with thistles and amphibious weeds,
Such as from earth's embrace the salt ooze breeds,
Is this ; an uninhabited seaside,
Which the lone fisher, when his nets are dried,
Abandons ; and no other object breaks
The waste, but one dwarf tree and some few stakes
Broken and unrepaired, and the tide makes
A narrow space of level sand thereon,
Where 'twas our wont to ride while day went down.
This ride was my delight.   I love all waste
And solitary places ; where we taste
The pleasure of believing what we see
Is boundless, as we wish our souls to be :
And such was this wide ocean, and this shore
More barren than its billows ;   .   .   .   .
.   .   .   . For the winds drove
The living spray along the sunny air
Into our faces ; the blue heavens were bare,
Stripped to their depths by the awakening north ;
And from the waves, sound like delight broke forth,
Harmonising with solitude, and sent
Into our hearts aërial merriment.

SHELLEY.

FROM "LINES WRITTEN AMONG THE EUGANEAN HILLS."

MANY a green isle needs must be
In the deep wide sea of misery,
Or the mariner, worn and wan,
Never thus could voyage on
Day and night and night and day,
Drifting on his dreary way,
With the solid darkness black
Closing round his vessel's track ;
Whilst above, the sunless sky,
Big with clouds, hangs heavily,
And behind the tempest fleet
Hurries on with lightning feet,
Riving sail, and cord, and plank,
Till the ship has almost drank
Death from the o'er-brimming deep ;
And sinks down, down, like that sleep
When the dreamer seems to be
Weltering through eternity ;
And the dim low line before
Of a dark and distant shore
Still recedes, as ever still
Longing with divided will,
But no power to seek or shun,
He is ever drifted on
O'er the unreposing wave,
To the haven of the grave.

SHELLEY.

FROM " REVOLT OF ISLAM."

III.

HARK ! 'tis the rushing of a wind that sweeps
Earth and the ocean.   See ! the lightnings yawn,
Deluging Heaven with fire, and the lashed deeps
Glitter and boil beneath : it rages on,
One mighty stream, whirlwind and waves upthrown,
Lightning, and hail, and darkness eddying by.
There is a pause—the sea-birds, that were gone
Into their caves to shriek, come forth, to spy
What calm has fall'n on earth, what light is in the sky.

IV.

For, where the irresistible storm had cloven
That fearful darkness, the blue sky was seen
Fretted with many a fair cloud interwoven
Most delicately, and the ocean green,
Beneath that opening spot of blue serene,
Quivered like burning emerald : calm was spread
On all below ; but far on high, between
Earth and the upper air, the vast clouds fled,
Countless and swift as leaves on autumn's tempest shed.

SHELLEY.

AND meet lone Death on the drear ocean's waste,
For well he knew that mighty Shadow loves
    The slimy caverns of the populous deep.

SHELLEY

FROM "QUEEN MAB."

THOSE trackless deeps, where many a weary sail
Has seen above the illimitable plain,
Morning on night, and night on morning rise,
Whilst still no land to greet the wanderer spreads
Its shadowy mountains on the sun-bright sea.
Where the loud roarings of the tempest-waves
So long have mingled with the gusty wind
In melancholy loneliness, and swept
The desert of those ocean solitudes,
But vocal to the sea-bird's harrowing shriek,
The bellowing monster, and the rushing storm,
Now to the sweet and many mingling sounds
Of kindliest human impulses respond.
Those lonely realms bright garden-isles begem,
With lightsome clouds and shining seas between,
And fertile valleys resonant with bliss,
Whilst green woods overcanopy the wave,
Which like a toil-worn labourer leaps to shore,
To meet the kisses of the flowrets there.

SHELLEY.

THE surf, like a chaos of stars, like a rout
Of death-flames, like whirlpools of fire-flowing iron,
With splendour and terror the black ship environ,
Or like sulphur-flakes hurl'd from a mine of pale fire
In fountains spout o'er it.

SHELLEY.

FROM "THE REVOLT OF ISLAM."

AND with it fled the tempest, so that ocean
And earth and sky shone through the atmosphere—
Only, 'twas strange to see the red commotion
Of waves like mountains o'er the sinking sphere
Of sun-set sweep, and their fierce roar to hear
Amid the calm : down the steep path I wound
To the sea-shore—the evening was most clear
And beautiful, and there the sea I found
Calm as a cradled child in dreamless slumber bound

SHELLEY.

TIME.

UNFATHOMABLE Sea ! whose waves are years !
  Ocean of Time, whose waters of deep woe
Are brackish with the salt of human tears !
  Thou shoreless flood which in thy ebb and flow
Claspest the limits of mortality,
And, sick of prey, yet howling on for more,
Vomitest thy wrecks on its inhospitable shore !
Treacherous in calm, and terrible in storm,
    Who shall put forth on thee,
      Unfathomable sea ?

SHELLEY.

IT is the unpastured sea hungering for a calm.

SHELLEY.

FROM " EPIPSYCHIDION."

THERE is a path on the sea's azure floor,
No keel has ever ploughed that path before ;
The halcyons brood around the foamless isles,
The blue Ægean girds this chosen home,
With ever-changing sound and light and foam
Kissing the sifted sands and caverns hoar ;
And all the winds wandering along the shore
Undulate with the undulating tide.

SHELLEY.

OR linger, where the pebble-paven shore,
(Under the quick, faint kisses of the sea)
Trembles and sparkles as with ecstacy.

SHELLEY.

HEAR I not

The Æolian music of our sea-green plumes ?

SHELLEY.

THE low lispings of the silvery seas.

P. J. BAILEY.

THE INCHCAPE ROCK.

No stir in the air, no stir in the sea,
The ship was still as she could be,
Her sails from heaven received no motion,
Her keel was steady in the ocean.

Without either sign or sound of their shock
The waves flowed over the Inchcape Rock ;
So little they rose, so little they fell,
They did not move the Inchcape Bell.

The worthy Abbot of Aberbrothok
Had placed that bell on the Inchcape Rock ;
On a buoy in the storm it floated and swung,
And over the waves its warning rung.

When the rock was hid by the surges' swell,
The mariners heard the warning bell ;
And then they knew the perilous rock,
And blest the Abbot of Aberbrothok.

The sun in heaven was shining gay,
All things were joyful on that day ;
The sea-birds screamed as they wheel'd round,
· And there was joyaunce in their sound.

The buoy of the Inchcape Bell was seen,
A darker speck on the ocean green ;

Sir Ralph the Rover walk'd his deck,
And he fixed his eye on the darker speck.

He felt the cheering power of spring,
It made him whistle, it made him sing ;
His heart was mirthful to excess,
But the Rover's mirth was wickedness.

His eye was on the Inchcape float ;
Quoth he, " My men, put out the boat,
And row me to the Inchcape Rock,
And I'll plague the Abbot of Aberbrothok.

The boat is lower'd, the boatsmen row,
And to the Inchcape Rock they go ;
Sir Ralph bent over from the boat,
And he cut the bell from the Inchcape float.

Down sank the bell with a gurgling sound,
The bubbles rose and burst around ;
Quoth Sir Ralph, "The next who comes to the Rock
Won't bless the Abbot of Aberbrothok."

Sir Ralph the Rover sail'd away,
He scour'd the seas for many a day ;
And now, grown rich with plunder'd store,
He steers his course for Scotland's shore.

So thick a haze o'erspreads the sky,
They cannot see the sun on high ;

The wind hath blown a gale all day,
At evening it hath died away.

On deck the Rover takes his stand,
So dark it is they see no land.
Quoth Sir Ralph, "It will be lighter soon,
For there is the dawn of the rising moon."

"Can'st hear," said one, "the breakers' roar?
For methinks we should be near the shore."
"Now where we are I cannot tell,
But I wish I could hear the Inchcape Bell!"

They hear no sound, the swell is strong;
Though the wind hath fallen they drift along,
Till the vessel strikes with a shivering shock,—
"Oh! heavens! it is the Inchcape Rock!"

Sir Ralph the Rover tore his hair,
He cursed himself in his despair;
The waves rush in on every side,
The ship is sinking beneath the tide.

But even now in his dying fear
One dreadful sound could the Rover hear,
A sound as if with the Inchcape Bell
The fiends in triumph were ringing his knell.

SOUTHEY.

LINES WRITTEN IN A LONELY BURIAL-GROUND IN THE HIGHLANDS.

How mournfully this burial-ground
Sleeps 'mid old Ocean's solemn sound,
Who rolls his bright and sunny waves
All round these deaf and silent graves !
The cold, wan light that glimmers here
The sickly wild flowers may not cheer ;
If here, with solitary hum,
The wandering mountain-bee doth come,
'Mid the pale blossoms short his stay,
To brighter leaves he booms away.
The sea-bird with a wailing sound
Alighteth softly on a mound,
And, like an image, sitting there
For hours amid the doleful air,
Seemeth to tell of some dim union,
Some wild and mystical communion,
Connecting with his parent sea
This lonesome stoneless cemetery.

*   *   *   *   *

Wild-screaming bird ! unto the sea
Winging thy flight reluctantly,
Slow floating o'er these grassy tombs
So ghost-like, with thy snow-white plumes,
At once from thy wild shriek I know
What means this place so steeped in woe !
Here, they who perish on the deep,
Enjoy at last unrocking sleep ;
For Ocean from his wrathful breast,

Flung them into this haven of rest,
Where shroudless, coffinless, they lie—
'Tis the shipwrecked seaman's cemetery.

*   *   *   *   *

Oh ! I could wail in lonely fear,
For many a woful ghost sits here,
All weeping with their fixed eyes !
And what a dismal sound of sighs
Is mingling with the gentle roar
Of small waves breaking on the shore ;
While Ocean seems to sport and play
In mockery of its wretched prey !

Here seamen old, with grizzled locks,
Shipwrecked before on desert rocks,
And by some wandering vessel taken
From sorrows that seem God-forsaken,
Home bound, here have met the blast
That wrecked them on death's shores at last !
Old friendless men, who had no tears
To shed, or any place for fears
In hearts by misery fortified,
And, without terror, sternly died.
Here many a creature moving bright
And glorious in full manhood's might,
Who dared with an untroubled eye
The tempest brooding in the sky,
And loved to hear that music rave,
And danced above the mountain-wave,
Hath quaked on this terrific strand,
All flung like sea-weeds to the land ;

A whole crew lying side by side,
Death-dashed at once in all their pride.
And here the bright-haired, fair-faced boy,
Who took with him all earthly joy,
From one who weeps both night and day
For her sweet son borne far away,
Escaped at last the cruel deep,
In all his beauty lies asleep ;
While she would yield all hopes of grace
For one kiss of his pale cold face !

And lo ! a white-winged vessel sails
In sunshine, gathering all the gales
Fast freshening from yon isle of pines
That o'er the clear sea waves and shines.
I turn me to the ghostly crowd,
All smeared with dust, without a shroud,
And silent every blue-swollen lip !
Then gazing on the sunny ship,
And listening to the gladsome cheers
Of all her thoughtless mariners,
I seem to hear in every breath
The hollow under-tones of death,
Who, all unheard by those who sing,
Keeps tune with low wild murmuring,
And points with his lean bony hand
To the pale ghosts sitting on this strand,
Then dives beneath the rushing prow,
Till on some moonless night of wo
He drives her shivering from the steep,
Down, down, a thousand fathoms deep.

John Wilson.

THE SHIPWRECK.

FROM " THE ISLE OF PALMS."

But list ! a low and moaning sound
At distance heard, like a spirit's song ;
And now it reigns above, around,
As if it called the ship along.
The moon is sunk ; and a clouded gray
Declares that her course is run,
And like a god who brings the day,
Up mounts the glorious sun.
Soon as his light has warmed the seas
From the parting cloud fresh blows the breeze ;
And that is the spirit whose well-known song
Makes the vessel to sail in joy along.
No fears hath she ; her giant form
O'er wrathful surge, through blackening storm,
Majestically calm would go
'Mid the deep darkness white as snow ;
But gently now the small waves glide
Like playful lambs o'er a mountain's side.
So stately her bearing, so proud her array,
The main she will traverse for ever and aye.
Many ports will exult at the gleam of her mast ;—
Hush ! hush ! thou vain dreamer ! this hour is her
Five hundred of souls in one instant of dread   [last,
    Are hurried o'er the deck ;
And fast the miserable ship
    Becomes a lifeless wreck.

Her keel hath struck on a hidden rock,
  Her planks are torn asunder,
And down come her masts with a reeling shock,
  And a hideous crash like thunder.
Her sails are draggled in the brine,
  That gladdened late the skies,
And her pendant, that kissed the fair moonshine,
  Down many a fathom lies ;
Her beauteous sides, whose rainbow hues
  Gleamed softly from below,
And flung a warm and sunny flush
  O'er the wreaths of murmuring snow,
To the coral rocks are hurrying down,
To sleep amid colours as bright as their own.
Oh ! many a dream was in that ship
  An hour before her death ;
And sights of home with sighs disturbed
  The sleeper's long-drawn breath.
Instead of the murmur of the sea,
The sailor heard the humming tree
  Alive through all its leaves,
The hum of the spreading sycamore
That grows before his cottage door,
  And the swallow's song in the eaves.
His arms enclosed a blooming boy,
Who listened with tears of sorrow and joy
  To the dangers his father had passed,
And his wife—by turns she wept and smiled,
As she looked on the father of her child,
  Returned to her heart at last.
He wakes at the vessel's sudden roll
And the rush of waters is in his soul.
Astounded the reeling deck he paces,
 Mid hurrying forms and ghastly faces ;

The whole ship's crew are there !
Wailings around and overhead,
Brave spirits stupefied or dead,
And madness and despair.

*　　*　　*　　*

Now is the ocean's bosom bare,
Unbroken as the floating air ;
The ship hath melted quite away,
Like a struggling dream at break of day.
No image meets my wandering eye,
But the new-risen sun and the sunny sky ;
Though the night-shades are gone, yet a vapour dull
Bedims the waves so beautiful :
While a low and melancholy moan
Mourns for the glory that hath flown.

JOHN WILSON.

FOAMS the wild beach below with maddening rage,
Where waves and rocks a dreadful combat wage.

WILLIAM FALCONER.

OCEAN is a mighty harmonist.

WORDSWORTH.

BY THE SEASIDE.

THE sun is couched, the sea-fowl gone to rest,
And the wild storm hath somewhere found a nest ;
Air slumbers—wave with wave no longer strives,
Only a heaving of the deep survives,
A tell-tale motion ! soon will it be laid,
And by the tide alone the water swayed.
Stealthy withdrawings, interminglings mild
Of light with shade in beauty reconciled—
Such is the prospect far as sight can range,
The soothing recompence, the welcome change.
Where now the ships that drove before the blast,
Threatened by angry breakers as they passed ;
And by a train of flying clouds bemocked ;
Or, in the hollow surge, at anchor rocked
As on a bed of death ?   Some lodge in peace,
Saved by His care who bade the tempest cease ;
And some, too heedless of past danger, court
Fresh gales to waft them to the far-off port,
But near, or hanging sea and sky between,
Not one of all those wingèd powers is seen,
Seen in her course, or 'mid this quiet heard ;
Yet oh ! how gladly would the air be stirred
By some acknowledgment of thanks and praise,
Soft in its temper as those vesper lays
Sung to the Virgin while accordant oars
Urge the slow bark along Calabrian shores ;
A sea-born service through the mountains felt

Till into one loved vision all things melt :
Or like those hymns that soothe with graver sound
The gulfy coast of Norway iron-bound;
And, from the wide and open Baltic rise,
With punctual care, Lutherian harmonies.
Hush, not a voice is here! but why repine,
Now when the star of eve comes forth to shine
On British waters with that look benign?
Ye mariners, that plough your onward way,
Or in the haven rest, or sheltering bay,
May silent thanks at least to God be given
With a full heart; " our thoughts are *heard* in
    heaven ! "

WORDSWORTH.

HAVE I not felt the longing
Then most intensely, when the storm-steed rushes
O'er the wild waves tumultuously thronging,
  Smiting their wan crests,—scattering as he crushes ;—
To stand on some lone peak, and hear, from under
Its caverned base, the ocean's melancholy thunder?

SIR AUBREY DE VERE.

THE storms and overwhelming waves
That tumble on the surface of the Deep.

COLERIDGE.

FROM "ON A HIGH PART OF THE COAST OF CUMBERLAND."

THE Sun, that seemed so mildly to retire,
Flung back from distant climes a streaming fire,
Whose blaze is now subdued to tender gleams,
Prelude of night's approach with soothing dreams.
Look round ;—of all the clouds not one is moving ;
'Tis the still hour of thinking, feeling, loving,
Silent, and steadfast as the vaulted sky,
The boundless plain of waters seems to lie :—
Comes that low sound from breezes rustling o'er
The grass-crowned headland that conceals the shore ?
No ; 'tis the earth-voice of the mighty sea,
Whispering how meek and gentle he *can* be !

WORDSWORTH.

FROM "BY THE SEA : EVENING."

IT is a beauteous evening, calm and free,
The holy time is quiet as a Nun
Breathless with adoration : the broad sun
Is sinking down in its tranquillity ;
The gentleness of heaven broods o'er the Sea :
Listen ! the mighty Being is awake,
And doth with his eternal motion make
A sound like thunder—everlastingly.

WORDSWORTH.

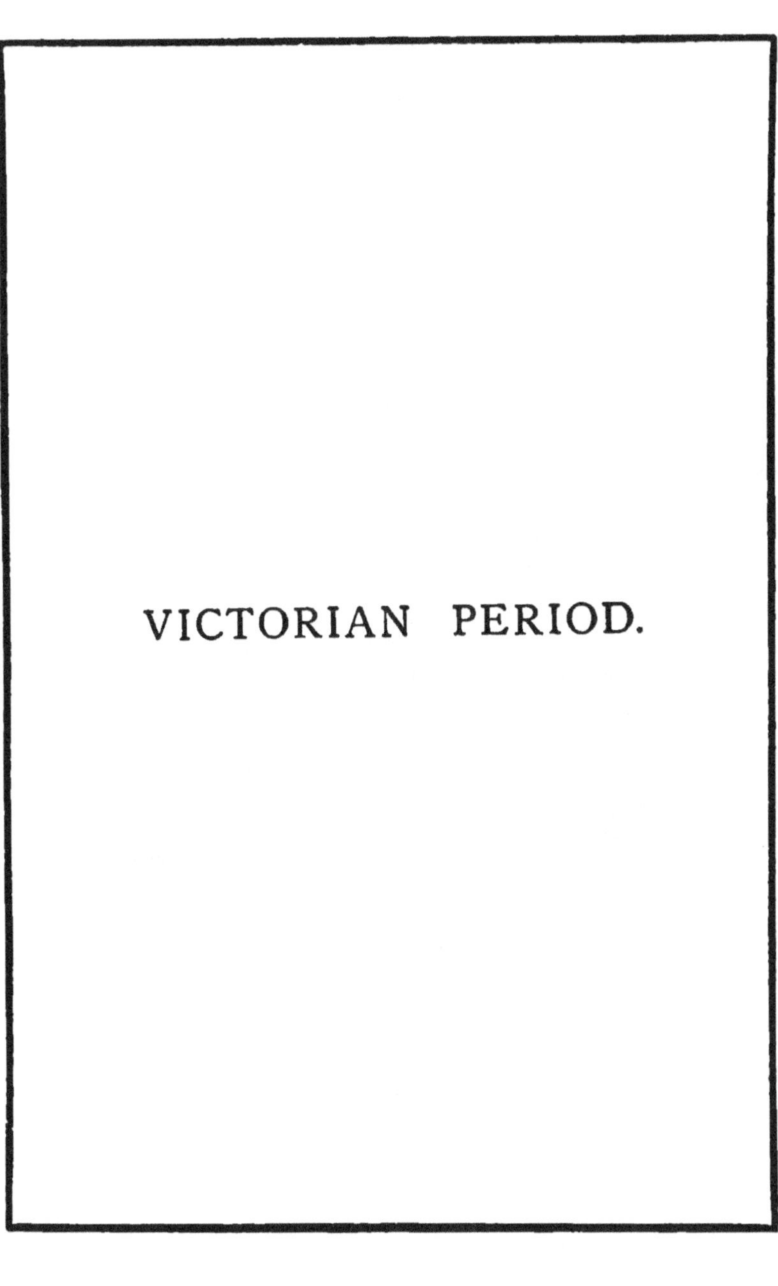

VICTORIAN PERIOD.

SEA DRIFT.

See where she stands, on the west sea sands,
    Looking across the water:
Wild is the night, but wilder still
    The face of the fisher's daughter.

What does she there in the light'ning's glare,
    What does she there, I wonder?
What dread demon drags her forth
    In the night and wind and thunder?

Is it the ghost that haunts this coast?—
    The cruel waves mount higher,
And the beacon pierces the stormy dark
    With its javelin of fire.

Beyond the light of the beacon bright
    A merchantman is tacking;
The hoarse wind whistling through the shrouds,
    And the brittle topmast cracking.

The sea it moans over dead men's bones,
    The sea it foams in anger;
The curlew swoop through the resonant air
    With a warning cry of danger.

The star-fish clings to the sea-weed's rings
    In a vague dumb sense of peril;

And the spray, with its phantom fingers, grasps
　At the mullein dry and sterile.

O, who is she that stands by the sea,
　In the light'ning's glare undaunted ?
Seems this now like the coast of Hell
　By one white spirit haunted !

The night draws by ; and the breakers die
　Along the ragged ledges ;
The robin stirs in its drenched nest,
　The hawthorn blooms on the hedges.

In shimmering lines, through the dripping pines
　The stealthy morn advances ;
And the heavy sea-fog straggles back
　Before those bristling lances !

Still she stands on the wet sea sands ;
　The morning breaks above her,
And the corpse of a sailor gleams on the rocks—
　What if it were her lover ?

T. B. ALDRICH.

A DAY-DREAM'S REFLECTION.

"ON THE SUNNY SHORE."

CHEQUER'D with woven shadows as I lay
Among the grass, blinking the watery gleam,
I saw an Echo-Spirit in his bay
Most idly floating in the noontide beam.
Slow heaved his filmy skiff, and fell, with sway
Of ocean's giant pulsing, and the Dream,
Buoyed like the young moon on a level stream
Of greenish vapour at decline of day,
Swam airily, watching the distant flocks
Of sea-gulls, whilst a foot in careless sweep
Touched the clear-trembling cool with tiny shocks,
Faint-circling; till at last he dropt asleep,
Lull'd by the hush-song of the glittering deep,
Lap-lapping drowsily the heated rocks.

WILLIAM ALLINGHAM.

THE FORSAKEN MERMAN.

COME, dear children, let us away ;
Down and away below !
Now my brothers call from the bay,
Now the great winds shoreward blow,
Now the salt tides seaward flow ;
Now the wild white horses play,
Champ and chafe and toss in the spray.
Children dear, let us away !
This way, this way !

Call her once before you go—
Call once yet !
In a voice that she will know :
" Margaret ! Margaret ! "
Children's voices should be dear
(Call once more) to a mother's ear ;
Children's voices, wild with pain—
Surely she will come again !
Call her once and come away :
This way, this way !
" Mother dear, we cannot stay !
The wild white horses foam and fret."
Margaret ! Margaret !

Come, dear children, come away down !
Call no more !
One last look at the white-wall'd town,

And the little grey church on the windy shore,
Then come down !
She will not come though you call all day ;
Come away, come away !

    Children dear, was it yesterday
We heard the sweet bells over the bay ?
In the caverns where we lay,
Through the surf and through the swell,
The far-off sound of a silver bell ?
Sand-strewn caverns, cool and deep,
Where the winds are all asleep ;
Where the spent lights quiver and gleam,
Where the salt weed sways in the stream,
Where the sea-beasts, ranged all round,
Feed in the ooze of their pasture-ground ;
Where the sea-snakes coil and twine,
Dry their mail and bask in the brine ;
Where great whales come sailing by,
Sail and sail, with unshut eye,
Round the world forever and aye ?
When did music come this way ?
Children dear, was it yesterday ?

    Children dear, was it yesterday
(Call yet once) that she went away ?
Once she sat with you and me,
On a red gold throne in the heart of the sea.
And the youngest sat on her knee.
She comb'd its bright hair, and she tended it well,

When down swung the sound of a far-off bell.
She sigh'd, she look'd up through the clear green sea ;
She said : " I must go, for my kinsfolk pray
In the little gray church on the shore to-day.
'Twill be Easter-time in the world—ah me !
And I lose my poor soul, Merman ! here with thee."
I said : " Go up, dear heart, through the waves !
Say thy prayer, and come back to the kind sea-caves ! "
She smiled, she went up through the surf in the bay.
Children dear, was it yesterday ?

Children dear, were we long alone ?
" The sea grows stormy, the little ones moan !
Long prayers," said I, " in the world they say.
Come ! " I said ; and we rose through the surf in the bay.
We went up the beach, by the sandy down
Where the sea-stocks bloom, to the white-wall'd town ;
Through the narrow paved streets, where all was still,
To the little gray church on the windy hill.
From the church came a murmur of folk at their prayers,
But we stood without in the cold blowing airs.
We climb'd on the graves, on the stones worn with rains,
And we gazed up the aisle through the small leaded panes.
She sat by the pillar ; we saw her clear ;
" Margaret, hist ! come quick, we are here.
Dear heart," I said, " we are long alone ;
The sea grows stormy, the little ones moan."
But ah, she gave me never a look,
For her eyes were seal'd to the holy book !
Loud prays the priest, shut stands the door.

F

Come away, children, call no more !
Come away, come down, call no more !

  Down, down, down !
Down to the depths of the sea !
She sits at her wheel in the humming town,
Singing most joyfully.
Hark what she sings : " O joy, O joy,
For the humming street, and the child with its toy !
For the priest, and the bell, and the holy well—
For the wheel where I spun,
And the blessed light of the sun ! "
And so she sings her fill.
Singing most joyfully,
Till the spindle drops from her hand,
And the whizzing wheel stands still.
She steals to the window, and looks at the sand,
And over the sand at the sea ;
And her eyes are set in a stare ;
And anon there breaks a sigh,
And anon there drops a tear,
From a sorrow-clouded eye,
And a heart sorrow-laden,
A long, long sigh ;
For the cold strange eyes of a little Mermaiden,
And the gleam of her golden hair.

  Come away, away children ;
Come, children, come down !
The hoarse wind blows colder ;

Lights shine in the town.
She will start from her slumber
When gusts shake the door ;
She will hear the winds howling,
Will hear the waves roar.
We shall see, while above us
The waves roar and whirl,
A ceiling of amber,
A pavement of pearl.
Singing : " Here came a mortal
But faithless was she !
And alone dwell forever
The kings of the sea."

But, children, at midnight,
When soft the winds blow,
When clear falls the moonlight,
When spring-tides are low ;
When sweet airs come seaward
From heaths starr'd with broom,
And high rocks throw mildly
On the blanch'd sands a gloom ;
Up the still, glistening beaches,
Up the creeks we will hie,
Over banks of bright sea-weed
The ebb-tide leaves dry.
We will gaze, from the sand-hills,
At the white, sleeping town ;
At the church on the hill-side—
And then come back down.

Singing : " There dwells a loved one,
But cruel is she !
She left lonely for ever
The kings of the sea."

Matthew Arnold.

FROM "DOVER BEACH."

The sea is calm to-night,
The tide is full, the moon lies fair
Upon the straits ;—on the French coast, the light
Gleams, and is gone ; the cliffs of England stand,
Glimmering and vast, out in the tranquil bay.
Come to the window, sweet is the night air !
Only, from the long line of spray
Where the ebb meets the moon-blanch'd sand,
Listen ! you hear the grating roar
Of pebbles which the waves draw back, and fling,
At their return, up the high strand,
Begin, and cease, and then again begin,
With tremulous cadence slow, and bring
The eternal note of sadness in.

Sophocles long ago
Heard it on the Ægean, and it brought
Into his mind the turbid ebb and flow
Of human misery ; we
Find also in the sound a thought,
Hearing it by this distant northern sea.

The Sea of Faith
Was once, too, at the full, and round earth's shore
Lay like the folds of a bright girdle furl'd ;
But now I only hear
Its melancholy, long, withdrawing roar,
Retreating to the breath
Of the night-wind down the vast edges drear
And naked shingles of the world.

MATTHEW ARNOLD.

FROM "STANZAS COMPOSED AT CARNAC.

FAR on its rocky knoll descried
   Saint Michael's chapel cuts the sky.
I climb'd ;—beneath me, bright and wide,
   Lay the lone coast of Brittany.

Bright in the sunset, weird and still,
   It lay beside the Atlantic wave,
As though the wizard Merlin's will
   Yet charm'd it from his forest-grave.

Behind me on their grassy sweep,
   Bearded with lichen, scrawl'd and gray,
The giant stones of Carnac sleep,
   In the mild evening of the May.

No priestly stern procession now
   Streams through their rows of pillars old ;

No victims bleed, no Druids bow ;
　Sheep make the daisied aisles their fold.

From bush to bush the cuckoo flies,
　The orchis red gleams everywhere ;
Gold furze with broom in blossom vies,
　The furze-scent perfumes all the air.

And o'er the glistening, lonely land,
　Rise up, all round, the Christian spires ;
The church of Carnac, by the strand,
　Catches the westering sun's last fires.

And there, across the watery way,
　See, low above the tide at flood,
The sickle-sweep of Quiberon Bay,
　Whose beach once ran with loyal blood !

And beyond that, the Atlantic wide !—
　All round, no soul, no boat, no hail ;
But, on the horizon's verge descried,
　Hangs, touch'd with light, one snowy sail !

Matthew Arnold.

And as the august blossom of the dawn
Burst, and the full sun scarce from sea withdrawn
Seemed on the fiery water a flower afloat.

A. C. Swinburne.

FROM " A SUMMER NIGHT."

HEADLANDS stood into the moon-lit deep
As clearly as at noon ;
The spring-tide's brimming flow
Heaved dazzlingly between ;
Houses with long white sweep
Girdled the glistening bay ;
Behind, through the soft air,
The blue haze-cradled mountains spread away.

*　　*　　*　　*　　*　　*

A few
Escape their prison, and depart
On the wide ocean of life anew.
There the freed prisoner, where'er his heart
Listeth, will sail ;
Nor doth he know how there prevail,
Despotic on that sea,
Trade-winds that cross it from eternity.
Awhile he holds some false way, undebarr'd
By thwarting signs, and braves
The freshening wind and blackening waves.
And then the tempest strikes him ; and between
The lightning-bursts is seen
Only a driving wreck,
And the pale master on his spar-strewn deck
With anguish'd face and flying hair,
Grasping the rudder hard,
Still bent to make some port he knows not where,
Still standing for some false impossible shore.
And sterner comes the roar
Of sea and wind, and through the deepening gloom

Fainter and fainter wreck and helmsman loom,
And he too disappears, and comes no more.

MATTHEW ARNOLD.

THE long lithe wave,
Now white-fringed, fretting into rough-curved bays,
Now swirling smoothly where flat sands gave
A couch whereon to end its stormy days.

ALFRED AUSTIN.

FEEBLE, shadowy, shallow? Is the ocean then shallow
    that keeps
Its harvest of shell and seaweed that none garners or
    reaps,
That the diver may sound a moment, but never drag
    from its deeps?

ALFRED AUSTIN.

SOON they were afresh upon the sea,
Hearing no more discordant tongues of men,
But only ocean's plastic melody,
With wave attuned to wave, attuned again
To wave, where every wave withal was free.

ALFRED AUSTIN.

ALL the running waves of eager life
End on the motionless fixed strand of death.

ALFRED AUSTIN.

FROM " THE HUMAN TRAGEDY."

BUT when a sunny sevennight had passed,
Up from the south there came a trailing cloud,
And in its train an ever-rising blast,
That soon was singing high in sail and shroud
And as it waxed, the sky grew overcast,
Lurid and low ;—whereat the breakers proud
Curved their strong crests, flung up their forelocks hoar,
And, madly rearing, plunged towards the shore.

And still as waned the day the wrathful ocean
Higher and higher rose, and to and fro
The slippery billows slid in shapeless motion,
Now dense now dark, now shivered into snow ;
Then once again as thick as hell-hag's potion
Clotted with briny litter from below :
Like leaden coffins yawning first to sight,
Then swiftly hidden with fringed shrouds of white.

And where the sun would have been seen to set,
If sun had been, the sky was darkened most,
And drooped the welkin lower and lower yet,
As night stole on without her starry host.
Anon, with flapping wings and stormy threat,
Foul seagulls came, and screamed along the coast ;
Then utter dark closed in before, behind,
And over all loud growled the wolfish wind.

ALFRED AUSTIN.

CLEAVE THOU THE WAVES.

CLEAVE thou the waves that weltering to and fro
Surge multitudinous.　The eternal Powers
Of sun, moon, stars, the air, the hurrying hours,
The winged winds, the still dissolving show
Of clouds in calm or storm, for ever flow
Above thee ; while the abysmal sea devours
The untold dead insatiate, where it lowers
O'er gloom unfathomed, limitless, below.

No longer on the golden-fretted sands,
Where many a shallow tide abortive chafes,
May'st thou delay ; life onward sweeping blends
With far-off heaven : the dauntless one who braves
The perilous flood with calm unswerving hands,
The elements sustain : cleave thou the waves.

MATHILDE BLIND.

CHRISTMAS EVE.

ALONE.—with one fair star for company,
  The loveliest star among the hosts of night,
  While the grey tide ebbs with the ebbing light—
I pace along the darkening wintry sea.
Now round the yule-log and the glittering tree
  Twinkling with festive tapers, eyes as bright
  Sparkle with Christmas joys and young delight,
As each one gathers to his family.

But I—a waif on earth where'er I roam—
  Uprooted with life's bleeding hopes and fears
From that one heart that was my heart's sole home,
  Feel the old pang pierce through the severing years,
And as I think upon the years to come
  That fair star trembles through my falling tears.

MATHILDE BLIND.

RETURN OF THE FISHING FLEET.

FROM "THE HEATHER ON FIRE."

HIGH on a granite boulder, huge in girth,
Primæval waif that owned a different birth
From all the rocks on that wild coast, alone,
Like some grey heron on as grey a stone,
And full as motionless, there stood a maid,
Whose sunbrowned hand her seaward eyes did shade
Flinching, as now the sun's auroral motion
Twinkled in milky ways on the grey heaving ocean.

Ah ! she had watched and waited overlong ;—
But now, as the new sunshine poured along
Heaven's hollow dome, till all its convex blue
Brimmed over as a harebell full of dew—
Yea, now she snatched the kerchief from her hair,
And waved its chequered tartan in the air ;
For all at once she heard o'er ocean's calm
The home-bound fishermen chanting King David's psalm.

In stormful straits, where battering craggy heights
Thundered the surf through equinoctial nights,
Off dolorous northern strands where loomed Cape Wrath
Red-lurid o'er the sea's unnatural math
Of goodly ships and men, or yet where lone
The Orkneys echoed to the tidal moan,
These men had plied their perilous task and rude,
Wrestling with wind and wave for scantiest livelihood.

Now laden they returned with finny spoil
The deep had tendered to their arduous toil ;
Their fishing smacks, with every black sail fanned
By favouring breezes, bore towards the land ;
And in their wake, or wheeling far away,
Or headlong dropping on the hissing spray,
Shrieked flocks of shore-birds, as now hove in sight
Fantastic cliffs and peaks a-bloom with morning light.

Ah ! dear as is her first-born's earliest lisp
To a young mother, toying with the crisp
Close rings that shine in many a clustering curl
Above the fair brow of her baby girl :
Or welcome, as when parted lovers meet
Their blissful looks and kisses,-- even so sweet
Unto the eyes of those sea-weary men
Gleamed old familiar sights of their own native glen :

The shallow stream wide-straggling on the beach,
That from cleft mountain ridges out of reach
Of aught save eagles, clattered from on high
To water the green strath and then to die
Merged in the deep ; the monstrous rocks that lay
Sharp-fanged like crocodiles agape for prey ;
The mushroom hovels pitch-forked on the strand,
Where browsed the small lean cattle mid the wet sea sand.

And from her perch the Highland lass had leapt,
Bounding from stone to stone ; while still she kept

Her footing on the slippery tangled mass
Through which her bare, brown, shapely feet did pass.
Nor was she now alone on that bleak shore,
For from each hut and corrie 'gan to pour
Women, old men, and children, come to greet
The fishers steering home their little herring fleet.

For now each boat was almost within reach,
Their keels were grating harshly on the beach ;
A rough lad here flung out his rope in coils,
There nets were cast ashore in whose brown toils
Live herrings quivered with a glint like steel,
Which, deftly shovelled into many a creel,
Were carried to the troughs.　And full of joy
The sailor hailed his wife, the mother kissed her boy.

MATHILDE BLIND.

A GREEN WAVE.

BETWEEN the salt sea-send before
　　And all the flowing gulfs behind,
　　Half lifted by the rising wind,
Half eager for the ungain'd shore,
A great green wave of shining light
Sweeps onward crowned with dazzling white.

Above, the east wind shreds the sky
With plumes from the grey clouds that fly.

WILLIAM SHARP.

THE STORM.

FROM "THE HEATHER ON FIRE."

THEN with his children Michael strode along,
His father followed through the elbowing throng
Of men and women, darting here and there
To snatch up children, or their household ware,
Splashing through sea-pools, stumbling over blocks,
To where the boats banged sharply on the rocks,
Bobbing like corks, and bearing from the shore
Their freight of human souls towards the *Koh-i-Noor*.

But as the shout of sailors, as the stroke
And dip of oars upon his senses broke,
The old man started back, and 'mid the loud
Din and confusion of the pushing crowd
He disappeared unnoticed, as the ship,
With many a lunge and shake and roll and dip,
Now weighed her anchors, and with bulging sail
Close-reefed, and creaking shrouds, drove on before the
    gale.

And crowding on the decks, with hungry eyes
Straining towards the coast that flies and flies,
The crofters stand ; and whether with tears or foam
The faces fastened on their dwindling home
Are wet, they know not, as they lean and yearn
Over the trickling bulwark by the stern
Toward each creek and headland of that shore,
The long-loved lineaments they may see never more.

Therewith it seemed as if their Scottish land
Bled for its children, yea, as though some hand—
Stretching from where on the horizon's verge
The rayless sun hung on the reddening surge—
Incarnadined the sweep of perilous coast,
And the embattled storm clouds' swarthy host,
With such wild hues of mingling blood and fire
As though the heavens themselves flashed in celestial ire.

And in the kindling of that wrathful light
Their huts, yet flaming up from vale and height,
Grew pale as watch-fires in the glare of day ;
White constellated isles leagues far away,
Headlands and reefs and paps whose fretted stone
Breasted the sucking whirlpool's clamorous moan,
Grew incandescent o'er the wind-flogged sea,
Scaled over with whitening scum as struck with leprosy.

For as the winds blew up to hurricane,
Like a mere spark quenched on the curdled main
The ship was swept beyond the old man's sight,
A dizzy watcher on that lonesome height,
Where grappled to a fragment of the keep,
He hung and swung high o'er the raging deep
While sea-gulls buffeted about his locks,
Slipped shrieking into chinks and crannies of the rocks.

And now the waves that thundered on the shore
Him seemed the iron-throated cannon's roar ;
And now his heart, upstarting as from sleep,

Shuddered for those that sailed upon the deep,
As in brief flashes of his clouded mind
He knew himself sole crofter left behind
Of all his clan—crying now and again,
" She's cleared the Sound of Sleat—safe on the open main.

" She's safe now, with the treacherous reefs behind !"
He shouted, as in answer to the wind
That had swung round like some infuriated host,
With all its blasts set full upon the coast ;
And hounded back, the ship, as if at bay,
Came reeling through the twilight, thick and grey
With rags of solid foam and shock of breaking
Waters,   beneath   whose   blows   the   very   rocks   were
      shaking.

Yea, near and nearer to the deadly shore
She pitches helpless 'mid the bellowing roar
Of confluent breakers, as with sidelong keel,
Dragging her anchors, she doth plunge and reel,
Dashed forwards, then recoiling from the rocks,
Whose flinty ribs ring to the Atlantic shocks—
On, on, and ever on, till hurled and battered
Sheer on the rock she springs, and falls back wrecked
      and shattered.

And through the smoke of waters and the clouds
Of driving foam, boats, rigging, masts, and shrouds
Whirled round and round ; and then athwart the storm
The old man saw, or raving saw, the form
Of his own son, as with his children pressed

G

Close to his heart, borne on the giddy crest
Of a sheer wall of wave, he rose and rose,
Then with the refluent surge rolled whelmed beneath its
    snows.

And through the lurid dusk and mist of spray
That quenched the last spark of the smouldering day,
Faces of drowning men were seen to swim
Amid the vortex, or a hand or limb
To push through whelming waters, or the scream
Wrung from a swimmer's choking lips would seem
 To be borne in upon the reeling brain
Of that old man, who swooned beneath the mortal
    strain.

Yea, thus once more upon the natal coast,
Which, living, those brave hearts had left and lost,
The pitying winds and waves drove back to land,
If but to drown them by the tempest's hand,
The banished Highlanders.   Safe in the deep,
With their own seas to rock their hearts to sleep,
The crofters lay : but faithful Rory gave
His body to the land that had begrudged a grave.

MATHILDE BLIND.

THE noise of seaward storm that mocks
With roaring laughter from reverberate rocks
The cry from ships near shipwreck.

A. C. SWINBURNE.

FROM "ST. ORAN."

ENTRANCED they gaze, and o'er the glimmering track
Of seething gold and foaming silver row :
Now to their left tower headlands, bare and black
And blasted, with grey centuries of snow,
Deep in whose echoing caves, with hollow sighs,
Monotonous seas for ever ebb and rise

*   *   *   *   *   *

The mountains opened wide on either hand,
And lo ! amid those labyrinths of stone
The sea had got entangled in the land,
And turned and twisted, struggling to get free,
And be once more the immeasurable sea.

MATHILDE BLIND.

THE deep divine dark dayshine of the sea,
Dense water-walls and clear dark water-ways,
Broad-based, or branching as a sea-flower sprays
That side or this dividing.

A. C. SWINBURNE.

BUT thou art terrible, with the unrevealed
Burden of dim lamentful prophecies,
And thy lone life is passionate and deep.

E. DOWDEN.

THE ROCK IN THE SEA.

THEY say that yonder rock once towered
    Upon a wide and grassy plain,
Lord of the land, until the sea
    Usurped his green domain :
Yet now remembering the fair scene
    Where once he reigned without endeavor,
The great rock in the ocean stands
    And battles with the waves for ever.

How oft, O rock, must visit thee
    Sweet visions of the ancient calm,
All amorous with birds and bees,
    And odorous with balm !
Ah me, the terrors of the time
    When the grim, wrinkled sea advances,
And winds and waves with direful cries
    Arouse thee from thy happy trances !

To no soft tryst they waken thee,
    No sunny scene of perfect rest,
But to the raging sea's vanguard
    Thundering against thy breast :
No singing birds are round thee now,
    But the wild wind, the roaring surges,
And gladly would they hurl thee down
    And mock thee in eternal dirges.

But be it thine to conquer them ;
  And may thy firm enduring form
Still frown upon the hurricane,
  Still grandly front the storm :
And while the tall ships come and go,
  And come and go the generations,
May thy proud presence yet remain
  A wonder unto all the nations.

Sometime, perchance, O lonely rock,
  Thou may'st regain thine ancient seat,
May'st see once more the meadow shine,
  And hear the pasture bleat :
But ah, methinks even then thy breast
  Would stir and yearn with fond emotion,
To meet once more in glorious war
  The roaring cohorts of the ocean.

HENRY AMES BLOOD.

THE shattered sun-gold of the main.

MATHILDE BLIND.

So long as sunn'd sea-waters round me pour
  Their saving strength—so long as I can hear
The thund'rous teachings of old ocean's lore
  And breathe salt breath, I dwell content of cheer.

WILLIAM CHARLES SCULLY.

BY THE SEA.

CHILDHOOD.

THERE comes to me a vision of the day
When first I made acquaintance with the sea
Rolling and rushing up the beach to me,
Then tumbling back, a giant in his play:
Lo! with arched neck again in foam and spray
Hoarse-voiced he leaps, recoils as speedily,
Leaving toyshells, his shining legacy,
Spars, pebbles, coral weeds of brightest ray.
Anon the many-mooded thing would sleep
In lamblike stillness all a summer noon,
While sunstars quivered on the hollow deep,
Then wake refreshed from slumber, and how soon
With wet and windy manes toss silver-bright,
A wilderness of motion and of light.

E. H. BRODIE.

THE BREAKERS.

PILING its dragon coils into a heap,
Far off, and yet inaudible, but dread,
The breaker rears its crested neck and head,
And now flings out in very act to leap
Its long upgathered bosom of the deep.
At once, like armèd men with earthquake tread,
Waved on through breach and gap, where Captain led,
O'er rock, up beach, swift unleashed waters sweep :
Rush ! roar ! recoil ! in froth, and flake, and foam,
Back, back they fall ; but clamorous of fight,
Pressed on by fresh battalions' fiercer rage,
So scours that nomad horde without a home,
Billows, that from lone Labrador took flight,
The war-hounds of old Atlas' unquelled age.

E. H. BRODIE.

TIDAL MUSIC.

Harmonious din, thee only that hour brings
When not an air is out upon the sea,
And silver waves slide o'er their velvet lea :
Night's music then, in the deep hush of things,
Thy voice is heard, crooning like one who sings
To some sick soul or cradled infancy,
Till sleep arriving close the lullaby,
Sleep with the fanning of his noiseless wings.
Swift muffled march of the returning tide,
Now louder with the freshening wind, but still
Free from hard discord, a melodious sound,
To thee I fling the casement open wide
This wintry night, to enter at thy will,
And steep me in forgetfulness profound.

E. H. Brodie.

FROM "FIFINE AT THE FAIR."

        I KEPT alive by man's due breath of air
I' the nostrils high and dry, at times o'er these would run
The ripple, even wash the wavelet,—for the sun
Tempted advance, no doubt : and always flash of froth,
Fish-outbreak, bubbling by, would find me nothing loth
To rise and look around ; then all was overswept
With dark and death at once.

    *   *   *   *   *

How quickly night comes !   Lo, already 'tis the land
Turns sea-like ! overcrept by grey, the plains expand,
Assume significance ; while ocean dwindles, shrinks
Into a better bound : its plash and plaint, methinks,
Six steps away, how both retire, as if their part
Were played, another force were free to prove her art,
Protagonist in turn !

ROBERT BROWNING.

THE grey sea and the long black land ;
And the yellow half moon large and low ;
And the startled little waves that leap
In fiery ringlets from their sleep
As I gain the cove with pushing prow
And quench its speed i' the slushy sand.

ROBERT BROWNING.

FROM "SORDELLO."

          CLIFFS, an earthquake suffered, jut
In the mid-sea, each domineering crest,
Nothing save such another throe can wrest
From out (conceive) a certain chokeweed growth
Since o'er the waters, twine and tangle thrown
Too thick, too fast accumulating round,
Too sure to over-riot and confound
Ere long each brilliant islet with itself
Unless a second shock save shoal and shelf,
Whirling the sea-drift wide : alas, the bruised
And sullen wreck ! Sunlight to be diffused
For that ! Sunlight, 'neath which a scum at first,
The million fibres of our chokeweed nurst
Dispread themselves, mantling the troubled main,
And, shattered by those rocks, took hold again,
So kindly blazed it—that same blaze to brood
O'er every cluster of the multitude
Still hazarding new clasps, ties, filaments,
An emulous exchange of pulses, vents
Of nature into nature ; till some growth
Unfancied yet, exuberantly clothe
A surface solid now, continuous, one.

ROBERT BROWNING.

STORM AND CALM.

THE lone House shakes, the wild waves leap around,
Their sharp mouths foam, their frantic hands wave high ;
I hear around me a sad soul of sound,—
   A ceaseless sob,—a melancholy cry.
   Above there is the trouble of the sky.
On either side stretch waters with no bound.
   Within, my cheek upon my hand, sit I,
Oft startled by sick faces of the drown'd.
   Yet are there golden dawns and glassy days
When the vast Sea is smooth and sunk in rest,
   And in the sea the gentle heaven doth gaze,
And, seeing its own beauty, smiles its best ;
   With nights of peace, when, in a virgin haze,
God's Moon wades through the shallows of the West.

R. BUCHANAN.

SEA-WASH.

WHEREFORE so cold, O Day,
  That gleamest far away
O'er the dim line where mingle heaven and ocean,
  While fishing-boats lie netted in the grey,
And still smooth waves break in their shoreward motion—
  Wherefore so cold, so cold?
  O say, dost thou behold
A Face o'er which the rock-weed droopeth sobbing,
  A Face just stirred within a sea-cave old
By the green water's throbbing?

  Wherefore, O Fisherman,
  So full of care and wan,
This weary, weary morning shoreward flying
  While stooping downward, darkly thou dost scan
That which below thee in thy boat is lying?
  Wherefore so full of care?
  What dost thou shoreward bear
Caught in thy net's moist meshes, as a token?
  Ah! can it be the ring of golden hair
Whereby my heart is broken?

  Wherefore so still, O Sea,
  That washest wearilie
Under the lamp lit in the fisher's dwelling,
  Holding the secret of thy deeps from me,
Whose heart would break so sharply at the telling?

Wherefore so still, so still ?
  Say, in thy sea-cave chill
Floats she forlorn with foam-bells round her breaking,
  While the wet fisher lands and climbs the hill
To hungry babes awaking !

ROBERT BUCHANAN.

FROM "CIRCE."

THE sun drops luridly into the west ;
Darkness has raised her arms to draw him down
Before the time, not waiting as of wont
Till he has come to her behind the sea ;
And the smooth waves grow sullen in the gloom
And wear their threatening purple ; more and more
The plain of waters sways and seems to rise
Convexly from its level of the shores ;
And low dull thunder rolls along the beach :
There will be storm at last, storm, glorious storm.

AUGUSTA WEBSTER.

A SHINING tract of ocean, where
Low winds with bland breaths flattered the mild air,
And low waves together did clasp and close,
And skyward yearning from the sea there rose
And seaward yearning from the sky there fell
A Spirit of Deep Content Unspeakable.

WILLIAM WATSON.

STORM.

FROM "MEG BLANE."

BLACK was the oozy lift,
  Black was the sea and land ;
Hither and thither, thick with foam and drift,
  Did the deep Waters shift,
Swinging with iron clash on stone and sand.
Faintlier the heavy Rain was falling,
Faintlier, faintlier the Wind was calling,
With hollower echoes up the drifting dark !
While the swift rockets shooting through the night
Flash'd past the foam-flecked reef with phantom light
And showed the piteous outline of the bark,
Rising and falling like a living thing
    Shuddering, shivering
While, howling beastlike, the white breakers there
Spat blindness in the dank eyes of despair.
Then one cried, " She has sunk ! "—and on the shore
Men shook, and on the heights the women cried ;
But, lo ! the outline of the bark once more,
While flashing faint the blue light rose and died.
Ah, God, put out Thy hand ! all for the sake
Of little ones, and weary hearts that wake,
Be gentle ! chain the fierce waves with a chain !
Let the gaunt seaman's little boys and girls
Sit on his knee and play with his black curls
    Yet once again !
And breathe the frail lad safely through the foam

Back to the hungry mother in her home !
And spare the bad man with the frenzied eye ;
Kiss him for Christ's sake, bid Thy Death go by—
   He hath no heart to die !

Now faintlier blew the wind, the thin rain ceased,
The thick cloud cleared like smoke from off the strand,
For, lo ! a bright blue glimmer in the East—
   God putting out His hand !
And overhead the rack grew thinner too,
   And through the smoky gorge
The Wind drave past the stars, and faint they flew,
   Like sparks blown from a forge !
And now the thousand foam-flames o' the Sea
   Hither and thither flashing visibly ;
And grey lights hither and thither came and fled,
Like dim shapes searching for the drownëd dead ;
And where these shapes most thickly glimmer'd by,
Out on the cruel reef the black hulk lay,
And cast against the kindling eastern sky,
Its shape gigantic on the shrouding spray.

Silent upon the shore, the fishers fed
Their eyes on horror, waiting for the close,
When in the midst of them a shrill voice rose :
   " The boat ! the boat ! " it said.
Like creatures startled from a trance, they turned
To her who spake ; tall in the midst stood she,
With arms uplifted, and with eyes that yearned
   Out on the murmuring sea.
Some, shrugging shoulders, homeward turned their eyes,
And others answered back in brutal speech ;
But some, strong-hearted, uttering shouts and cries,
Followed the fearless woman up the beach.

A rush to seaward—black confusion—then
A struggle with the surf upon the strand—
'Mid shrieks of women, cries of desperate men,
The long oars smite, the black boat springs from land !
   Around the thick spray flies ;
The waves roll on and seem to overwhelm.
With blowing hair and onward gazing eyes
The woman stands erect and grips the helm. . . .
Now fearless heart, Meg Blane, or all must die !
Let not the skill'd hand thwart the steadfast eye !
The crested wave comes near,—crag-like it towers
Above you, scattering round its chilly showers :
One flutter of the hand, and all is done !
Now steel thy heart, thou woman-hearted one !
   Softly the good helm guides ;
Round to the liquid ridge the boat leaps light, -
Hidden an instant,—on the foaming height,
Dripping and quivering like a bird, it rides.
Athwart the ragged rift the Moon looms pale,
   Driven before the gale
And making silvern shadows with her breath,
Whereon the sighing sea it shimmereth ;
And, lo ! the light illumes the reef; 'tis shed
Full on the wreck, as the dark boat draws nigh.
A crash !—the wreck upon the reef is fled ;
A scream !—and all is still beneath the sky
Save the wild waters as they whirl and cry.

ROBERT BUCHANAN.

FAR beneath
Sleepeth the glassy ocean like a sheet
Of liquid mother-o'-pearl, and on its rim
A ship sleeps, and the shadow of the ship ;
Astern the reef juts darkly, edged with foam,
Thro' the smooth brine: oh, hark ! how loudly sings
A wild, weird ditty to a watery tune,
The fisher among his nets upon the shore ;
And yonder, far away, his shouting bairns
Are running, dwarf'd by distance small as mice,
Along the yellow sands.

ROBERT BUCHANAN.

THE INCOMING TIDE.

GREY-GLIMMERING thro' the dusky air
    The spectral cliffs loom o'er the sea,
    And up the strand tumultuously
The windy tidal billows tear :
How stern yon rock—nay, look once more,
The heedless waves above it pour !

Borne inwards o'er the spray-swept land
In thunder booms the sea's command.

WILLIAM SHARP.

H

FROM "THE LIFTING OF THE VEIL."

I SAW below me
The glassy ocean
　　Glimmering,
With a white sail dipping
Against the azure
　　Like a sea-bird's wing—
And all looked pleasant,
　　On sea and land,
The white cloud brooding,
And the white sail dipping,
And the village sitting
　　On the yellow sand.

And beside the waters
My Soul saw the fishers
Staring upward,
　　With dumb desire
Tho' a mile to seaward,
With the gulls pursuing,
Shot past the herring
　　With a trail like fire ;
Though the mighty Sea-snake
With her young was stranded
In the fatal shallows
　　Of the shingly bay.

ROBERT BUCHANAN.

O what is this moaning so faint and low,
  And what is this crying from night to morn ?
The moaning is that of the souls that go,
  The crying is that of the souls new born.
The life-sea gathers with stormy calls,
  The wind blows shrilly, the foam flies free.
The great wave rises, the great wave falls,
  I swim to its height by the side of thee !
With arms outstretching and throats that scream,
  With faces that flash into foam and fly,
Our beings break in the light of a dream,
  As the great waves gather and die.

ROBERT BUCHANAN.

And constant shells that evermore retain
The moody music of the murmuring main.

RICHARD GARNETT.

With desperate longing, more than foam which lies
Splashed up awhile where the cold spray descries
  The waves whereto their cold limbs were resigned ;
  Yet ever doth the sea-winds undefined
Vague wailing shudder with their dying sighs.

OLIVER MADOX BROWN.

FROM "BALDER THE BEAUTIFUL."

                                   LONG hours he paced
The cold sands of the still black sea ; and where
His foot fell moonlight lay and live sea-snails
Crept glimmering with pink horns ; and close to shore
He saw the legions of the herring flash,
Swift, phosphorescent, on the surface shining
Like bright sheet-lightning as they came and went.
At intervals, from the abyss beyond,
Came the deep roar of whales.

                                  Betimes he stood
Silent, alone upon a promontory.
And now about him like white rain there fell
The splendour of the moonlight.   All around
The calm sea rolled upon the rocks, or drew
Dark surges from the caverns, issuing thence
Troubled and churn'd to boiling pools of foam.

                                     ROBERT BUCHANAN.

                              AFTER trouble there was peace ;
Smooth, many-coloured, as a ringdove's neck,
Stretch'd the deep, and on its eastern rim
The cool, sweet light, with yellow rainy beams,
Gleamed like a sapphire.   Overhead, soft airs
To feathery cirrhus flecked the deepening blue ;
Beneath, the smooth seas breathing made a breeze ;
And up the weedy beach the blue waves crept,
Breaking in one thin line of creamy foam.

                                     ROBERT BUCHANAN.

THE HAUNTED SHORE.

I WALK'D at sunset by the lonely waves,
When Autumn stood about me, gold and brown ;
I watch'd the great red sun, in clouds, go down,
An orient King, that 'mid his bronzèd slaves
Dies, leaning on his sceptre, with his crown.
A hollow moaning from innumerous caves,
In green and glassy darkness sunk below,
Told of some grand and ancient deed of woe,
Of murdered kings that sleep in weltering graves.
Still thro' the sunshine wavering to and fro,
With sails all set, the little vessels glide ;
Mild is the Eve and mild the ebbing Tide,
And yet that hollow moaning will not go,
Nor the old Fears that with the sea abide.

WILLIAM M. W. CALL.

FROM "A NIGHT'S RHAPSODY."

No night for slumber is this—
A night to be up and away
Where the sea is rolled in a tide of gold
Under the full moon's ray;
To fly with the wind till the cleft waves hiss
From the racing prow each way,
Where the tumult of winds and of waters is
Over the sounding bay.
And the sails in the moonlight shine,
The flashing foam flies free,
The land is a long low line,
The gunwale scoops the brine,
And the air is stronger than wine,
And lords of the night are we.

H. E. CLARKE.

ALL night by the shore.

The obscure water, the long white lines of advancing foam—the rustle and thud, the panting sea-breaths, the sea-smell—

The great slow air moving from the distant horizon—the immense mystery of space, and the soft canopy of the clouds.

EDWARD CARPENTER.

AT MIDNIGHT OF ALL SOULS.

I HEAR the rushing of the sea of Time,
　Whose mighty waters in their pauseless whelm,
　Suck down, resistless, nation, race, and realm,
Like rotting sea-weed, drench'd in ooze and slime.
Ocean ! incarnardin'd with countless crime,
Green with drown'd hopes, and wreck of joyous prime ;
　Salt with the myriad tears of human woes ;
　Toss'd with the surge and tumult of earth's throes ;
We note thy shifting sands, and pace thy shore,
We watch thy ebbing tides, and list thy roar,
　Heark'ning, with awe, th' innumerable things
　Told in thy billowy thunderings ;
Until by the coming of our one appointed wave,
We're swept into th' eddy of that universal grave.

MARY COWDEN CLARKE.

FROM "THE FLYING DUTCHMAN."

STILL southward—through the torrid seas,
  Past surf-bound tufts of palms,
And witched in waters where no breeze
  Stirs the tranced zone of calms.
Where all the sails drooped dead, and low
  The listless pennant hung,
And round and round, and to and fro,
  The vessel idly swung.

With stooping masts—with decks foam-strewn,
  And prow wrapped white in spray
She fled before the fierce monsoon,
  A hundred leagues a day ;
While writhing shafts came stalking o'er
  The deep in whirling routs,
And sky and sea were roof and floor
  To aisles of water-spouts.

Still southward through the lengthening days
  And lingering twilights dim,
Till morn chased midnight with its rays
  Behind the ocean's rim.
And fleets of icebergs sailed in files,
  Tall phantoms pale in shrouds,
Till seemed the sea thus thronged for miles,
  A firmament of clouds,

And like the clouds where Heaven breaks through
  Their shining folds of white,
Those fronts of ice were veined with blue
  Where lifted to the light.
Some stooped their polished flanks to lean
  O'er bases burrowed through,
Scooped by the wave in arches green,
  Or infinitely blue.

They soared in flames to meet the day,
  As through the ocean burned—
Or quench'd in twilight's ashen grey,
  To livid corpses turned.
The noonday sun their summits smote
  With pale prismatic sheen,
Or clothed them, like the peacock's throat,
  In woven blue and green.

A spectral army northward driven
  The self-same path for years,
They reared against the verge of Heaven,
  A host of silver spears.
And sometimes clashed in battle shock,
  Like Titans in the lists,
And hurled in thunder cliff and rock,
  Through rising ocean mists.

*   *   *   *   *

The gust brought up a pall for night,
  And tore her veil away,
The tattered shreds of mist took flight,
  And settled o'er the bay.

The ship was folded in a cloud,
  From earth, and sea, and sky ;
And no man's glance has pierced that shroud,
  Save when his end was nigh.

Resounding to the thunder's din,
  Down stooped the dark, as though
The arch of heaven were falling in,
  On all things here below.
Its roof in rifts of glory broke,
  Abyss flamed into height,
And the dead heart of midnight woke,
  Convulsed, in throbs of light.

The void profound was stirred with sound,
  And quick with stings of fire,
And echoing far from star to star,
  Pealed heaven's tremendous choir.
Those flaming shafts whose torment wrung
  All secrets from the dark,
Pierced not the shield of shadow flung
  Around the fated bark.

But when the wrath of the typhoon,
  In devastating sweep,
With midnight in its heart at noon,
  Is loosed upon the deep,
And in its clutches onward whirled,
  All helpless and forlorn,

With naked spars and canvas furled,
  Some crippled ship is borne.

Drowned deep in spray, the destined prey
  Of ocean's gaping jaws,
Still blindly stumbling on her way,
  With many a dizzy pause,
She sees a vessel tall with sail,
  Uplifted as a tower,
Drive like a cloud before the gale,
  Yet stoop not to its power ;

With drift on drift of snowy cloth,
  Wreathed high on mast and spar
Tempting the hurricane's wild wrath,
  Swift as a shooting star.
The waters smoke—the whirlwinds wake,
  Their chaos is her home,
And from her prow in lightnings break
  The splintered sheaves of foam.

A wraith along the deep she goes,
  Till nearing swift and pale,
Upon the fated wreck she throws
  The shadow of her sail.
And through the storm with hollow chime
  A spectral hail they hear,
" How goes the world ? Methinks 'twere time
  That Doomsday should appear ! "

E. M. CLERKE.

BY THE SEA.

On either hand
A sweep of tawny sand
With gentle curve extending, smooth and wide,
On which bold rocks look down
With dark and sullen frown,
Slopes out to meet the fast incoming tide.

The sunbeams leap
And frolic o'er the deep,
And where their light is most intensely pour'd,
Strike from its surface keen
Flashes of diamond sheen,
Dazzling the eyes that gaze out thitherward.

A cloud or two
Drifts lightly 'mid the blue ;
And, like a faint white blot upon the sky,
Up yonder you can trace
The day moon's dim drowned face,
Whose light will flood all heaven by-and-by.

The rythmical
Hoarse sounds that rise and fall,
Thund'rous, upon the ear from out at sea,
The tumult nearer land,
And splash upon the sand
Of breaking waves, compose one harmony.

Elsie Cooper.

THE STORMY PETREL.

WHEN fierce along his ocean-path
The North wind rushes in his wrath,
And down the vast, insatiate wave
The great ship shudders to her grave,
Whence is it that thy tiny form
Exults, and challenges the storm?

Oh, not for thee the bloom-sweet gales
Of orchards ; or in thymy vales
The bee's low hum : the rush and roar
Of breakers on some savage shore,
Or organ-winds through sea-caves blown,
Are harmonies for thee alone !

Man's argosies are swept to naught ;
Yet o'er the havoc, tempest-wrought,
Companion of the wandering sea—
Tumult and Death but toy with thee,
And cheer thee in thy lonely flight,
Making our horror thy delight !

Oh, would, strange bird, I too could sweep
Unharmed along life's angry deep,
Nor heed the lowering clouds that roll
And darken round the struggling soul—
Like thee could soar, and breast, elate,
The mists of doubt, the storms of fate !

HENRY S. CORNWELL.

IN THE DAY OF THE EAST WIND.

THE rocks at my feet are strewn with crimson and brown
    seaweed
Brought by the tidal swell, as waves after waves succeed,
And break with a plash in my path, but I do not heed ;
  And over the Links comes the east wind drearily moan-
    ing.

I stand on the edge of the rock-pool, and gaze into it, and
    why ?
The place has a strange fascination for me, but not one
    of those am I
Who would seek a self-sought grave in its depth, de-
    spairingly ;
  And over the Links comes the east wind drearily moan-
    ing.

I have put the temptation from me, but it comes back
    again and again,
That I should quiet, in this way, the aching of heart and
    of brain,
And the sea always whispers, "Come," with its eerie,
    surging refrain,
  And over the Links comes the east wind drearily moan-
    ing.

Homeward I go through the shingle and sand, while the
    spray of the sea
Fills my hair with the salt ooze and foam, and the billows
    break ceaselessly,
Rolling in with resistless force, like some dark-coming
    Destiny ;
  And over the Links comes the east wind drearily moan-
    ing.

BESSIE CRAIGMYLE.

SEA-PICTURES.

I.—MORNING.

THE morning sun has pierced the mist,
And beach and cliff and ocean kissed.
Blue as the lapis-lazuli
The sea reflects the azure sky.
In the salt healthy breeze I stand
Upon the solid floor of sand.
Along the untrodden floor are seen
Fresh tufts of weed, maroon and green ;
And ruffled kelp with stranded sticks
And shells and stones and sea-moss mix.
The low black rocks for ever wet
Lie tangled in their pulpy net.
The shy sand-pipers fly and light :
The swallows circle out of sight :
And on the horizon blue afar
Each white sail glimmers like a star.
Old Ocean smiles as though amid
His leagues of brine no treachery hid.
And safe upon the sandy marge
By stranded boat and floating barge,
Gay children leap and laugh and run,
Browned by the salt air and the sun.

CHRISTOPHER P. CRANCH.

SEA-PICTURES.

II.—EVENING.

Now thickening twilight presses down
Upon the harbour and the town ;
And all around a misty pall
Of dull gray cloud hangs over all.
The huddling fishing-sloops lie safe ;
While far away the breakers chafe.
And now the landsman's straining eye
Mingles the gray sea and the sky.
Far out upon the darkening deep
The white ghosts of the ocean leap.
Boon-Island light, a lonely star,
Is flashing o'er the waves afar.
Upon the beach the sea rolls in,
In never-ending foam and din ;
And all along the craggy shore
Resounds one long continuous roar.
We turn away to hail each gleam
Where lamps from cottage windows stream.
For sad and solemn is the moan
Of ocean when the day has flown,
And borne on dusky wings, the night
Wraps in a shroud the dying light.

Christopher P. Cranch.

THE SETTING OF THE MOON NEAR CORINTH.

From that dejected brow in silence beaming
A light it seems too feeble to retain,
A sad calm tearful light through vapours gleaming,
Slowly thou sinkest on the Ægean main ;
To me an image, in thy placid seeming,
Of some fair mourner who will not complain ;
Of one whose cheek is pale, whose eyes are streaming,
Whose sighs are heaved unheard,—not heaved in vain.
  And yet what power is thine ! as thou dost sink,
Down sliding slow along that azure hollow,
The great collected Deep thy course doth follow,
Amorous the last of those faint smiles to drink ;
And all his lifted fleets in thee obey
The symbol of an unpresuming sway !

Aubrey De Vere.

EVENING, NEAR THE SEA.

Light ebbs from off the Earth; the fields are strange,
  Dark, trackless, tenantless; now the mute sky
  Resigns itself to Night and Memory,
And no wind will yon sunken clouds derange,
No glory enrapture them; from cot or grange
  The rare voice ceases; one long-breathëd sigh,
  And steeped in summer sleep the world must lie;
All things are acquiescing in the change.
Hush! while the vaulted hollow of the night
  Deepens, what voice is this the sea sends forth,
    Disconsolate iterance, a passionless moan?
Ah! now the Day is gone, and tyrannous Light,
  And the calm presence of fruit-bearing Earth:
    Cry, Sea! it is thy hour; thou art alone.

EDWARD DOWDEN.

THE MORNING SEA.

CRADLED in sapphire mist, Morn's sunlit Deep
   Wakes the whole world with laughter, darkness past,
   And with immeasurable music cast
Shoreward, 'mid sighs of strange relationship,
Earth's wandering mystic kinsman loves to keep
   Her ear attent with mystery to the last,—
   Whilst, like sea-butterflies with wings shut fast,
White ships walk summer seas in stately sleep.

Here fondling mother-like the pink-lipped shell,
   That pearly grot or bubbling fountain paves,
Rocking the cradle of the asphodel,—
Yet all the while thou'rt thundering evermore,
   With multitudinous hosts of armèd waves,
Loud at the gates of Thule's utmost shore !

CHARLES A. FOX.

SEA VOICES.

I.

ART thou the voice of God, thou tremulous Sea,
Surrounding with eternal melody
Earth's strong foundations, trembling thro' her caves,
And with the warning voice of thy blind waves
Dost murmur prophecies of things to be,
When Earth no more shall plant upon the sea
Her foot of rock, but conquering sea again
Shall stream his billowy banners over men?
Dost murmur prophecies of things to come,
When wandering Ocean shall disclose the tomb
Of kings and heroes and all living souls,
Whose winding-sheet thou stretchest from the poles,
Whilst o'er them thine eternal anthem rolls?
Art thou the voice of God, thou tremulous Sea,
Or but the echo of eternity?

II.

But whence that human voice, serene, divine,
Above the roar of tempests blent with thine,
Most wondrous work of God, mysterious Sea?
Heaven's mightiest wonderworks Christ wrought on thee,
Secrets of strength told none but Galilee!
Who that first saw thee couched along the shore,
Sleepy with sunshine, durst suspect thy roar—
When roused from liquid lair in glorious haste
Thou boundest o'er the immeasurable waste,

Storm-wreathed and thundering !—fleeing solitudes
Flash thy foam-fury to Earth's utmost roods,
Hurling to heaven thy wrath's stupendous praise,
So grandly infinite are all thy ways !
Or who e'er saw thee crouching with mute smile,
Waiting to waft whole fleets to some far isle,
Mightiest of creatures, but forgot the while—
How without signal, bursting on the sight,
Huge mountain ranges, leaping height o'er height,
Ride plunging in, majestic in their might,—
Whilst, borne aloft like dread suspended powers,
O'er dirging wastes charge leagues of foaming towers
Toiling to storm Earth's pale beleaguered shores !
Or singled from the innumerable host,
Like desperate courier fled from worlds just lost,
With smoking crest flung maddening to the sky,
Lone towering dread like smoky Sinai,
Some breathless billow thunders in to die !
Who durst compare his single voice to thee,
Thunder of mighty waters ? Only He
Who strode thy fierce crests, startled Galilee !
Though powers tempestuous yoked thy chariot-throne,
One rode thee once whose magic word alone
Reined thee to instant stillness at a groan—
'Mid thy storm-trampled fury's darkest rage
He wrote in light Truth's calmest, tenderest page !

CHARLES A. FOX.

WHERE CORALS LIE.

THE deeps have music soft and low
  When winds awake the airy spry,
It lures, lures me on to go
  And see the land where corals lie.

By mount and mead, by lawn and rill,
  When night is deep, and moon is high,
That music seeks and finds me still,
  And tells me where the corals lie.

Yes, press my eyelids close, 'tis well ;
  But far the rapid fancies fly
To rolling worlds of wave and shell,
  And all the land where corals lie.

Thy lips are like a sunset glow,
  Thy smile is like a morning sky,
Yet leave me, leave me, let me go
  And see the land where corals lie.

RICHARD GARNETT.

THE BALLAD OF THE BOAT.

THE stream was smooth as glass, we said : " Arise and
    let's away ; "
The Siren sang beside the boat that in the rushes lay ;
And spread the sail, and strong the oar, we gaily took
    our way.
When shall the sandy bar be cross'd ?   When shall we
    find the bay ?

The broadening flood swells slowly out o'er cattle-dotted
    plains,
The stream is strong and turbulent, and dark with heavy
    rains,
The labourer looks up to see our shallop speed away.
When shall the sandy bar be cross'd ? When shall we find
    the bay ?

Now are the clouds like fiery shrouds ; the sun, superbly
    large,
Slow as an oak to woodman's stroke sinks flaming at
    their marge.
The waves are bright with mirror'd light as jacinths on
    our way.
When shall the sandy bar be cross'd ? When shall we find
    the bay ?

The moon is high up in the sky, and now no more we
    see
The spreading river's either bank, and surging distantly
There booms a sullen thunder as of breakers far away.
Now shall the sandy bar be cross'd, now shall we find the
    bay !

The sea-gull shrieks high overhead, and dimly to our
    sight
The moonlit crests of foaming waves gleam towering
    through the night.
We'll steal upon the mermaid soon, and start her from
    her lay,
When once the sandy bar is cross'd, and we are in the
    bay.

What rises white and awful as a shroud-enfolded ghost ?
What roar of rampant tumult bursts in clangour on the
    coast ?
Pull back, pull back ! The raging flood sweeps every
    oar away.
O stream, is this thy bar of sand ? O boat, is this the
    bay ?

RICHARD GARNETT.

THE sea complains upon a thousand shores

ALEXANDER SMITH.

.THE MERMAID OF PADSTOW.

IT is long Tom Yeo of the town of Padstow,
    And he is a ne'er-do-weel :
" Ho ! mates," quoth he, " rejoice with me,
    For I have shot a seal."

Nay, Tom, by the mass thou art but an ass,
    No seal bestains this foam ;
But the long wave rolls up a Mermaid's glass,
    And a young Mermaiden's comb.

The sun hath set, the dark clouds throng,
    The sea is steely gray :
They hear the dying Mermaid's song
    Peal from the outer bay.

" A curse with ye go, ye men of Padstow,
    Ye shall not thrive or win :
Ye have seen the last ship from your haven slip,
    And the last ship enter in.

For this deed I devote ye to dwell without boat,
    By the skirt of the oarèd sea,
And ever be passed by sail and by mast,
    And none with an errand for ye."

And scarce had she spoke when the black storm
    broke,
    With thunder and levin's might :

Three days did it blow, and none in Padstow
  Could tell the day from night.

Joy ! the far thunder mutters soft,
  The wild clouds whirl o'erhead,
And from a ragged rift aloft
  A shaft of light is sped.

Now ho ! for him that waits to send
  The storm-bound bark to sea,
And ho ! for them that hither bend
  To crowd our busy quay.

Hath Ocean, think ye then, not heard
  His dying child deplore?
Are not his sandy deeps upstirred,
  And thrust against the shore?

Doth not a mighty ramp of sand
  Beleaguer all the bay,
Mocking the strength of human hand
  To pierce or sweep away?

The white-winged traders all about
  Fare o'er that bar to win ;
But this one cries, " I cannot out,"
  And that, " I may not in."

For thy dire woe, forlorn Padstow,
  What remedy may be?

Not all the brine of thy sad eyne
   Will float thy ships to sea.

The sighs that from thy seamen pass
   Might set a fleet a-sail;
And the faces that look in the Mermaid's glass
   Are as long as the Mermaid's tail.

RICHARD GARNETT.

THE dim star of the ocean lieth cool
In palpitating silver, while beneath
Her image, putting luminous feelers forth,
Bathes liquid, like a living thing o' the sea.

ROBERT BUCHANAN.

THE water's in stripes like a snake, olive-pale
   To the leeward,—
On the weather-side black, spotted white with the wind.

ROBERT BROWNING.

EARTH and sky and ocean held their breath
In reverence.   Only by fits the sea,
As though impatient of the enchanted calm,
Like a chained monster in reluctant rest,
Gave out a wearied moan.

SIR NOEL PATON.

TO THE WEST !

I WEEP, for I am weary—no faint dreaming,
Through mist and heat and noises of the town,
Will ever bring to the silver-gleaming
    Cool sea below the Down.

The purple shells in deep rock waters hide them,
And dip, and lave themselves beneath the sea,—
But nevermore in the western wind beside them
    Shall waves wash over me.

Far, far below the crags in sunshine sleeping,
Beneath the slippery grass, the boulders grey,—
The great sea in the midday hush is creeping,
    And gulls laugh in the bay.

They laugh across the bay,—whose quiet plashing
Echoes,—the wind bears murmurs of the sea
Ev'n down deep summer lanes, where bells are clashing,
    And far-off voices be.

At nightfall, when the low-voiced tide is crossing
Over lone sands by Thirleston's weedy door,—
Out in the darkened sea the boats are tossing,
    And winds sigh off the shore.

But I weep, for I am weary—no faint dreaming
Through mist and heat and noises of the town,
Can ever bring me to that silver-gleaming
　　　　Cool sea below the Down.
　　　　　　　　　ALICE E. GILLINGTON.

AND the rainbow lives in the curve of the sand ;
Hither, come hither, and see ;
And the rainbow hangs on the poising wave,
And sweet is the colour of cove and wave.
　　　　　　　　　LORD TENNYSON.

THE BRIDE'S PRELUDE.

NIGHT lapsed.　At dawn the sea was there
　　And the sea-wind : afar
The ravening surge was hoarse and loud,
And underneath the dim dawn cloud
Each stalking wave shook like a shroud.
　　　　　　　　　D. G. ROSSETTI.

How from the excavating tide they* win
A voice poetic, solacing though sad,
Which, when the passionate winds revisit them,
Gives utterance to the injuries of time.
　　　　　　　　　HENRY TAYLOR.

---

* The rocks.

VIGIL.

THE kittiwake hangs on the seaward cliff,
The cormorant skirts the wave,
While here I sit in my lonely skiff,
At the mouth of the green sea-cave.
O soft little waves, run lightly in,—
The melody sweet you sing
Has never an echo of storm-wind's din,
And winter-night's sorrowing.

Play and plash on the shell-strewn sand,
Your tribute of weeds lay down,
Shining wet on the shimmering strand,
Purple, and gold, and brown,—
Let all your ripples be filled with song,
Your scattering foam-crests fly
Like dropping laughter the whole day long
In measureless ecstasy.

For every pleasure that comes with spring,—
And every joy that wakes
In the quiet doing of some quaint thing
Observed for the old sakes' sakes,—
And every bliss that my heart yet knows,
Shall melt and vanish away,
Absorbed in the rapture that overflows
To-morrow—my wedding-day!

MARY C. GILLINGTON.

A WAVE.

O WILD grey rocks, O weed green rocks, O white rocks
    wet with spray,
By happy waters washed all night, by sunbeams kissed
    all day,—
Among your rifts a little wave has strayed and lost its
    way.

Hither it runs, and thither roves—but all the gates are
    fast ;
Where is the echoing entrance now through which at
    first it passed ?
It beats at every outlet whence it *may* escape at last.

"O stay with us," the rocks besought, "for bleak
    though we be and bare,
We have never so small a crevice but a wave may
    shelter there,
And tell us tales of its deep sea-home, of the ocean far
    and fair."

They locked the wave in their wild brown arms, they
    wooed it like a bride,
But minute by minute it dwindled there, it sank in the
    sands and died ;
And ever it heard with fainter ears the voice of the
    waves outside.

The hot sun sucked it up above, the dry sand drank
    below ;—
And in the shadow of rugged rocks, more lost it sank
    and low ;
It died, what time the first small star looked out of the
    afterglow.

M. C. GILLINGTON.

O WILD black Sea that flashes fitful light
Against the sullen shadow of the night,
Whose heaving waters through the twilight call,
And thunder up against the harbour wall,—-
To thee alone, the lost, the comfortless
May cry aloud in their supreme distress :
Thy voice replies, love tender, pity deep,
Through the dead midnight ; when the world's
    asleep.

M. C. GILLINGTON.

O FAR away, green waves, your voices call,
Your cool lips kiss the wild and weedy shore ;
And out upon the sea-line, sails are brown ;
White sea-birds, crying, hover—soft shades fall,
Deep waters dimple round the dripping oar,
And last rays light the little fishing town.

M. C. GILLINGTON.

THE SONG OF THE SURF.

WHITE steeds of ocean, that leap with a hollow and
    wearisome roar
On the bar of ironstone steep, not a fathom's length from
    the shore,
Is there never a seer nor sophist can interpret your wild
    refrain,
When speech the harshest and roughest is seldom studied
    in vain ?
My ears are constantly smitten by that dreary mono-
    tone,
In a hieroglyphic 'tis written—'tis spoken in a tongue
    unknown ;
Gathering, growing, and swelling, and surging, and
    shivering, say !
What is the tale you are telling? What is the drift of
    your lay?

You come, and your crests are hoary with the foam of
    your countless years ;
You break, with a rainbow of glory, through the spray
    of your glittering tears.
Is your song a song of gladness? a pœan of joyous
    might ?
Or a wail of discordant sadness for the wrongs you never
    can right ?
For the empty seat by the ingle? for children 'reft of
    their sire ?
For the bride, sitting, sad, and single, and pale, by the
    flickering fire ?

K

For your ravenous pools of suction? for your shattering
    billow swell?
For your ceaseless work of destruction? for your hunger
    insatiable?

Not far from this place, on the sand and the shingle dry,
He lay with his batter'd face upturn'd to the frowning
    sky.
When your waters wash'd and swill'd high over his
    drowning head,
When his nostrils and lungs were fill'd, when his feet and
    hands were as lead,
When against the rock he was hurl'd, and suck'd under
    again to the sea,
On the shores of another world, on the brink of eternity,
On the verge of annihilation, did it come to that swim-
    mer strong,
The sudden interpretation of your mystical, weird-like
    song?

Mortal! that which thou askest, ask not thou of the waves;
Fool! thou foolishly taskest us—we are only slaves;
Might, more mighty, impels us—we must our lot fulfil,
He who gathers and swells us curbs us too at His will.
Thinkest thou the wave that shatters questioneth His
    decree?
Little to us it matters, and naught it matters to thee.
Not thus murmuring idly, we from our duty would
    swerve,
Over the world spread widely, ever we labour and serve.

ADAM LINDSAY GORDON.

THE SWIMMER.

WITH short, sharp, violent lights made vivid,
　To southward far as the sight can roam,
Only the swirl of the surges livid,
　The seas that climb and the surfs that comb.
Only the crag and the cliff to nor'ward,
And the rocks receding, and reefs flung forward,
And waifs wreck'd seaward and wasted shoreward
　On shallows sheeted with flaming foam.

A grim, grey coast and a seaboard ghastly,
　And shores trod seldom by feet of men—
Where the batter'd hull and the broken mast lie,
　They have lain embedded these long years ten.
Love ! when we wander'd here together,
Hand in hand through the sparkling weather,
From the heights and hollows of fern and heather,
　God surely loved us a little then.

The skies were fairer and shores were firmer—
　The blue sea over the bright sand roll'd ;
Babble and prattle, and ripple and murmur,
　Sheen of silver and glamour of gold—
And the sunset bath'd in the gulf to lend her
A garland of pinks and of purples tender,
A tinge of the sun-god's rosy splendour,
　A tithe of his glories manifold.

Man's works are graven, cunning, and skilful
   On earth where his tabernacles are ;
The sea is wanton, the sea is wilful,
   And who shall mend her and who shall mar ?
Shall we carve success or record disaster
On her bosom of heaving alabaster ?
Will her purple pulse beat fainter or faster
   For fallen sparrow or fallen star ?

*   *   *   *   *

So, girt with tempest and wing'd with thunder
   And clad with lightning and shod with sleet,
And strong winds treading the swift waves under
   The flying rollers with frothy feet.
One gleam like a bloodshot sword-blade swims on
The skyline, staining the green gulf crimson,
A death-stroke fiercely dealt by a dim sun
   That strikes through his stormy winding sheet.

Oh ! brave white horse ! you gather and gallop,
   The storm sprite loosens the gusty reins ;
Now the stoutest ship were the frailest shallop
   In your hollow backs, on your high-arched manes.
I would ride as never a man has ridden
In your sleepy, swirling surges hidden,
To gulfs foreshadow'd through strifes forbidden,
   Where no light wearies and no love wanes.

ADAM LINDSAY GORDON.

FROM "ON THE CLIFF."

Down drops the red sun ; through the gloaming
   They burst—raging waves of the sea
Foaming out their own shame—ever foaming
   Their leprosy up with fierce glee ;
Flung back from the stone, snowy fountains
   Of feathery flakes, scarcely flag
Where, shock after shock, the green mountains
   Explode on the iron-grey crag.

     *   *   *   *   *   *

The gale has gone down ; yet outlasting
   The gale, raging waves of the sea
Casting up their own foam, ever casting
   Their leprosy up with wild glee,
Still storm ; so in rashness and rudeness
   Man storms through the days of his grace ;
Yet man cannot fathom God's goodness,
   Exceeding God's infinite space.

ADAM LINDSAY GORDON.

Round the cape of a sudden came the sea,
And the sun looked over the mountain's rim,
And straight was a path of gold for him,
And the need of a world of men for me.

ROBERT BROWNING.

FROM "THE PAINTER."

SUMMER has done her work ; she, lingering, sees
  Her shady places glare : yet cooler grow
The breezes as they stir the sunny trees,
  Whose shaking twigs their ruby berries sow.
Ripe is the fairy-grass, we breathe its seeds.
  But, hanging o'er the rocks that belt the shore,
  Safe from the sea, above its bustling roar,
Here ripen, still, the blossom-swinging weeds.

Pale cressets on the summer waters shine,
  No ripple there but flings its jet of fire.
Rich amber wrack still bronzing in the brine
  Is tossed ashore in daylight to expire.
A wallowing wave the rocky shoal enwreathes ;
  From the loose spray, cascades of bubbles fall
  Down steeps whose watery, coral-mantled wall
Drinks of the billow, and the sunshine breathes.

Summer has done her work, but mine remains.
  How shall I shape these ever murmuring waves,
How interweave these rumours and refrains,
  These wind-tossed echoes of the listening caves ?
The restless rocky roar, the billow's splash,
  And the all-hushing shingle—hark ! it blends,
  In open melody that never ends,
The drone, the cavern-whisper, and the clash.

And this wild ruin of a once new shore
  Scooped by new waves to waves of solid rock,
Dark-shelving—white-veined, as if marbled o'er
  By the fresh surf still trickling block by block !
O worn-out waves of night, long set aside—
  The moulded storm in dead, contending rage,—
  Like monster-breakers of a by-gone age !
And now the gentle waters o'er you ride.

Can my hand darken in swift rings of flight
  The air-path cut by the black sea-gull's wings,
Then fill the dubious track with influent light,
  While to my eyes the vanished vision clings?
While at their sudden whirr the billows start,
  Can my hand hush the cymbal-scunding sea,
  That breaks with louder roar its reverie
As those fast pinions into silence dart?

Press on, ye summer waves, still gently swell,—
  The rainbow's parent-waters over-run !
Can my poor brush your snaky greenness tell,
  Raising your sheeny bellies to the sun?
What touch can pour you in yon pool of blue
  Circling with surging froth of liquid snow,
  Which now dissolves to emerald, now below
Glazes the sunken rocks with umber hue ?

Summer has done her work, dare I begin—
  Painting a desert, though my pencil craves
To intertwine all tints with heaven akin?
  Nature has flung her palette to the waves !

Then bid my eyes on cloudy landscape dwell,—
  Not revel in thy blaze.   O beauteous scene !
  Between thy art and mine is nature's screen,—
Transparent only to the soul,—farewell !

T. GORDON HAKE.

THE sense of vastness, when at night
We hear the roll and dash of waves that break
Nearer and nearer with the rushing tide, ·
Which rises to the level of the cliff
Because the wide Atlantic rolls behind,
Throbbing respondent to the far-off orbs.

GEORGE ELIOT.

BREAKING BILLOWS.

A SKY of whirling flakes of foam,
  A rushing world of dazzling blue ;
  One moment, the sky looms in view—
The next, a crash in its curv'd dome,
A tumult indescribable,
And eyes dazed with the miracle.

Here breaks by circling day and night,
In thunder, the sea's boundless might.

WILLIAM SHARP.

FROM "THE BIRTH OF VENUS."

THE waters of the warm, surf-laden sea,
   Couched 'neath a heaven of love that o'er them
Lie trance-bound in a dream of ecstasy,   [bends,
   Prophetic of a rapture that impends.

Now they swell up as if love's underflow
   Lifted their bosom, the sun's shredded fires
Glinting each tremor ; now, with pulses low,
   They lapse into a deluge of desires.

The sun glares on its way along the deep,
   And, bounding to the zenith's utmost height,
There vacillates and from his fiery steep
   Burns in his pride on ocean to alight.

The procreative ether downward floats
   On slanting beams that pierce the dazzled sky,
And nature kindles as the vivid motes
   With crackling germs her rage beatify.

     *   *   *   *   *   *

The sun has sunk, in his voluptuous heat
   Creaming with rosy love the ocean floor,
Till only serried waves his blush repeat,
   As they uprise and froth the pulpy shore.

The stars revolve in pairs, the fiery red
   Infect the deathly pale with new desires,

The rocks whose climbing paths the welkin reach,
    Lashed by the waves, with foam are overrun.

Mermaids lie dead along the wreck-strewn sands,
    Pitched by high waves upon the ocean-side,
With snapt-off boughs of coral in their hands,—
    Their scaly folds frothed in the panting tide.

Over the quiet sea rides on his back
    The sun-stained dolphin, there in lifeless ease,
Tossed up and down 'mid isles of bladder-wrack
    Wrenched with their shell-fish from the weeded seas.

But in one bay held by the nymphs that bathe
    In its translucent pools and trust to view
Their dripping hair and bosom, while they swathe
    Their waists in coral spangled by the dew,

Or twist green garlands round them for a shrine,
    Culling the briny flowers with pearl inwove,
That unctuous cling as tendrils of a vine,
    And weave a bower for newly-budded love ;—

In such a bay where bluest waters buoy
    Leaves coral-strown and froth of bubbling white,
Where the dipped rays o'er shallow rocks deploy
    And film soft honeycombs of shaking light;—

Lo ! there bright golden ringlets interlace,
    A rosy hand athwart a bosom gleams,

Then sweeps the surf; and thence looks forth a face
  As if at length inheriting its dreams.

                              T. GORDON HAKE.

THE tide comes rolling in in ridgy sheets,
Surge after surge, with hollow-bosomed roar,
Plunges and breaks, then hurriedly retreats,
And the stunned strand stands solid as before.
But swift a fresh on-coming billow meets
The flying foam, and carries it along,
Back to the assault, with volume doubly strong.

                              ALFRED AUSTIN.

THAT day of days when I and you
  Stood by the sea whose stormy shallows roared
On wastes of shell-strewn sand?   The sky was blue
  As down the hot sun on the wet sand poured,
Up streamed the sea-scent warm, and sharp, and sweet,
We laughed to see the billows thundering meet.

None, save us twain, upon the shore was seen,
  The gull cried loud his short hard stormy cry,
The blown foam crested all the deep sea's green,
  The summer sun burnt hot, the wind was high,
Up hissing dashed the bright spray in our eyes
When a great wave broke with a great surprise.

                              PHILIP B. MARSTON.

TO A SEA-BIRD.

SAUNTERING hither on listless wings,
　　Careless vagabond of the sea,
Little thou heedest the surf that sings,
The bar that thunders, the shale that rings,—
　　Give me to keep thy company.

Little thou hast, old friend, that's new,
　　Storms and wrecks are old things to thee ;
Sick am I of these changes, too ;
Little to care for, little to rue,—
　　I on the shore and thou on the sea.

All of thy wanderings, far and near,
　　Bring thee at last to shore and me ;
All of my journeyings end them here,
This our tether must be our cheer,—
　　I on the shore and thou on the sea,

Lazily rocking on ocean's breast,
　　Something in common, old friend, have we ;
Thou on the shingle seek'st thy nest,
I to the waters look for rest,—
　　I on the shore and thou on the sea.

BRET HARTE.

GREYPORT LEGEND.

THEY ran through the streets of the seaport town ;
They peered from the decks of the ships where they lay ;
The cold sea-fog that came whitening down
Was never as cold or white as they.
  " Ho, Starbuck and Pinckney and Tenterden !
Run for your shallops, gather your men,
  Scatter your boats on the lower bay."

Good cause for fear ! In the thick midday
The hulk that lay by the rotting pier,
Filled with the children in happy play,
Parted its moorings and drifted clear ;
  Drifted clear beyond reach or call—
  Thirteen children there were in all—
  All adrift in the lower bay !

Said a hard-faced skipper, " God help us all !
She will not float till the turning tide !"
Said his wife, " My darling will hear *my* call,
Whether in sea or Heaven she bide."
  And she lifted a quavering voice and high,
  Wild and strange as a sea-bird's cry,
  Till they shuddered and wondered at her side.

The fog broke down on each labouring crew,
Veiled each from each and the sky and shore ;

There was not a sound but the breath they drew,
And the lap of water and creak of oar ;
   And they felt the breath of the downs, fresh blown
   O'er league of clover, and cold grey stone,
   But not from the lips that had gone before.

They come no more, but tell the tale
That, when fogs are thick on the harbour reef,
The mackerel fishers shorten sail,
   For the signal they know will bring relief,—
   For the voices of children, still at play
   In a phantom hulk that drifts alway
   Through channels whose waters never fail.

It is but a foolish shipman's tale,
A theme for a poet's idle page,
But still when the mists of doubt prevail,
And we lie becalmed by the shores of age,
   We hear from the misty troubled shore
   The voice of the children gone before,
   Drawing the soul to its anchorage.

BRET HARTE.

WHERE a dim sea-presence broodeth in solemn sullen
   state—
Where no mortal breath dare whisper, only hollow sounding surges,
A welter of wild waters with their melancholy dirges.

HON. RODEN NOEL.

"PATER VESTER PASCIT ILLA."

Our bark is on the waters ! wide around,
The wandering wave ; above, the lonely sky :
Hush ! a young sea-bird floats, and that quick cry
Shrieks to the levelled weapon's echoing sound :
Grasp its lank wing, and on, with reckless bound !
Yet, creature of the surf, a sheltering breast
To-night shall haunt in vain thy far-off nest,
A call unanswered search the rocky ground.
      Lord of Leviathan ! when Ocean heard
Thy gathering voice, and sought his native breeze ;
When whales first plunged with life, and the proud
    deep
Felt unborn tempests heave in troubled sleep,
Thou didst provide, even for this nameless bird,
Home and a natural love amid the surging seas.

Robert Stephen Hawker.

THE WESTERN SEA.

I SAW thee on a summer's day
 Among the many isles asleep;
A few faint fleecy cloudlets lay
 In shadow on thine azure deep;
And as they drifted past, I knew
How bright and boundless was the blue.

I saw thee pitiless and cold,
 With clouds and darkness overcast;
Long stormy crested billows rolled
 Before an icy northern blast:
And broke far off with ceaseless shocks
On bleak inhospitable rocks.

I had not loved thy sleep so well,
 If wintry winds had never blown:
I learned of thy tempestuous swell
 The music of thy softer tone:
And when the waves were dark as night,
I blest thy paths of rippling light.

E. G. A. HOLMES.

L

NIGHT.

Night comes and stars their wonted vigils keep
  In soft unfathomable depths of sky :
  In mystic veil of shadowy darkness lie
The infinite expanses of the deep,—
Save where the silvery paths of moonlight sleep,
  And rise and sink for ever dreamily
  With the majestic heaving of the sea.
Night comes, and tenfold gloom where dark and steep,
Into black waters of a land-locked bay
The cliffs descend : there never tempest raves
  To break the awful slumber ; far below
  Glimmer the foamy fringes white as snow ;
And sounds of strangled thunder rise alway,
And midnight moanings of imprisoned waves.

E. G. A. Holmes.

LOOP HEAD.

A SHEER surf-beaten island fronts the shore
　Close to the headland cliffs, whence stormy waves
　Have rent it : there the sea imprisoned raves
Between dark dungeon walls, and evermore
Deep in that chasm, with sullen booming roar,
　Comes surging in a rushing raging tide,
　That pants and boils, and climbs each dripping side,
Then sinks as madly as it rose before.
Beyond, bright crests of ocean waves are tost
　Into the far faint haze that ends the view :
Northward, the headlands of a rocky coast
　Are white with surf—while southward, broad and blue,
The Shannon rolls, in tranquil majesty,
Into the billows of the boundless sea.

E. G. A. HOLMES.

LISCANNOR BAY.

Two walls of precipices black and steep,
  The storm-lashed ramparts of a naked land,
  Are parted here by leagues of lonely sand
That make a bay ; and up it ever creep
Billowy ocean ripples half asleep,
  That cast a belt of foam along the strand,
  Seething and white, and wake in cadence grand
The everlasting thunder of the deep.
And there is never silence on that shore—
  Alike in storm and calm foam-fringes gird
Its desolation, and the Atlantic's roar
  Makes mighty music.   Though the sea be stirred
By scarce a breath of breeze, yet evermore
  The sands are whitened, and the thunder heard.

E. G. A. Holmes.

LIGHT AND SHADE.

Too deeply blue ! Too beautiful ! Too bright !
  Oh ! that the shadow of a cloud might rest
  Somewhere upon the splendour of thy breast
In momentary gloom : the molten light
That hides thy far horizon pains my sight :
  Too crystal clear thy waves that heave below
  O'er green rocks fathoms deep : the fringing snow
That girds thy headland cliffs is all too white.
So as I mused, a sudden turn revealed
  The dungeon gloom of a cliff-circled bay,
Where the sad sea, whose wounds are never healed,
  Makes moan of muffled thunder night and day,—
And awful shadows sleep, and all things seem
Dark and mysterious as an evil dream.

E. G. A. HOLMES.

A WAVE.

O BEING in thy dissolution known
　　Most lovely then ;
O Life that ever has to die alone,
　　To live again ;
O bounding Heart that still must bow and break
　　To touch thine end ;
O broken Purpose that must failure take,
　　And deathward bend,
For the great tide to stretch from rock to rock
　　His shining way ;
O wandering Will that from the furthest shock
　　Of sea-deeps grey,
Silver constraint of secret light on high
　　Lead safe to shore ;
O living Rapture that dost inly sigh,
　　And evermore
Within thy joy the wailful voices keep ;
　　I see thee now,
O Son of the unfathomable deep !
　　And trembling know
The crownèd Shadow of man's opposites,
　　The forces dread
That sway him into being, blanched with lights
　　Of thunder bred ;
A poisèd Passion wrought from central breath
　　Of whirling storms,
And evermore a deathless life in death,
　　That still re-forms.

And thou, man's prototype in varying moods,
    Didst lonely beat
The vacant shores and speechless solitudes
    With silver feet,
Through the great æons wandering forlorn
    In search of him,
As rose and fell like vacant flames, lone morn
    And evening dim,
Ere light had grown articulate in love,
    Or silence knew
Herself as worship.   Then didst thou ever move
    Beneath the blue,
An incommunicable mystery,
    About thy shore ;
A visible yearning of earth and sea,
    That evermore
Flung out white arms to catch at some far good
    Yet unfulfilled,
And failing sobbed and sank in solitude
    With heart unstilled ;
A voice that ever crying as of old
    In deserts dumb,
With hollow tongue reverberate foretold
    A Life to come.

ELLICE HOPKINS.

. . . I WOULD sail upon the tropic seas,
  Where fathom long the blood-red dulses grow,
Droop from the rock and waver in the breeze,
  Lashing the tide to foam ; while calm below
The muddy mandrakes throng those waters warm,
And purple, gold, and green, the living waters swarm.

JEAN INGELOW.

BY THE SEA.

I WALKED with her I love by the sea,
  The deep came up with its chanting waves,
Making a music so great and free
    That the will and the faith, which were dead in me,
      Awoke and rose from their graves.

Chanting, and with a regal sweep
  Of their broidered garments, up and down
The strand came the mighty waves of the deep,
    Dragging the wave-worn drift from its sleep
      Along the sea-sands bare and brown.

" O my soul, make the song of the sea ! " I cried,
  " How it comes, with its stately tread,
And its dreadful voice, and the splendid pride
    Of its regal garments flowing wide
      Over the land ! " to my soul I said.

My soul was still ; the deep went down.
  " What hast thou, my soul," I cried,
" In thy song ? " " The sea-sands bare and brown,
  With broken shells and sea-weed strown
    And stranded drift," my soul replied.

WILLIAM DEAN HOWELLS.

FROM "COOGEE" (AUSTRALIA).

SING the song of wave-worn Coogee—Coogee in the distance white
With its jags and points disrupted, gaps and fractures
fringed with light !
Haunt of gledes and restless plovers of the melancholy
wail
Ever lending deeper pathos to the melancholy gale.

There, my brothers, down the fissures, chasms deep and
wan and wild,
Grows the sea-bloom, one that blushes like a shrinking
fair blind child ;
And amongst the oozing forelands many a glad green
rock-vine runs,
Getting ease on earthy ledges sheltered from December
suns.

Often, when a gusty morning, rising cold and gray and
strange,
Lifts its face from watery spaces, vistas full with cloudy
change ;
Bearing up a gloomy burden which anon begins to wane,
Fading in the sudden shadow of a dark determined rain ;

Do I seek an eastern window, so to watch the breakers
beat
Round the steadfast crags of Coogee, dim with drifts of
driving sleet ;
Hearing hollow mournful noises sweeping down a solemn
shore
While the grim sea-caves are tideless and the storm
strives at their core.

HENRY KENDALL.

ARAKOON.

Lo, in storms, the triple-headed
    Hill, whose dreaded
Bases battle with the seas,
Looms across fierce widths of fleeting
    Waters beating
Evermore on roaring leas !

Arakoon, the black, the lonely !
    Housed with only
Cloud and rain-wind, mist and damp :
Round whose foam-drenched feet, and nether
    Depths, together
Sullen sprites of thunder tramp !

There the East hums loud and surly,
    Late and early,
Through the chasms and the caves ;
And across the naked verges
    Leap the surges !
White and wailing waifs of waves.

Day by day, the sea-fogs gathered—
    Tempest-fathered—
Pitch their tents on yonder peak !
Yellow drifts and fragments, lying
    Where the flying
Torrents chafe the cloven creek !

And at nightfall, when the driven
    Bolts of heaven
Smite the rock, and break the bluff,
Thither troop the elves whose home is
    Where the foam is,
And the echo, and the clough.

Ever girt about with noises,
    Stormy voices,
And the salt breath of the strait,
Stands the steadfast Mountain Giant,
    Grim, reliant,
Dark as Death, and firm as Fate !

So when trouble treads, like thunder,
    Weak men under—
Treads, and breaks the thews of these—
Set thyself to bear it bravely,
    Greatly, gravely,
Like a hill in yonder seas :

Since the wrestling, and endurance,
    Give assurance
To the faint at bay with pain,
That no soul to strong Endeavour
    Yoked for ever,
Works against the tide in vain.

HENRY KENDALL.

THE THREE FISHERS.

THREE fishers went sailing away to the West,
   Away to the West as the sun went down ;
Each thought on the woman who loved him best,
   And the children stood watching them out of the town ;
For men must work, and women must weep,
And there's little to earn, and many to keep,
     Though the harbour-bar be moaning.

Three wives sat up in the lighthouse tower,
   And they trimm'd the lamps as the sun went down ;
They look'd at the squall, and they look'd at the shower,
   And the night-rack came rolling up ragged and brown.
But men must work, and women must weep,
Though storms be sudden, and waters deep,
     And the harbour-bar be moaning.

Three corpses lay out on the shining sands
   In the morning gleam as the tide went down,
And the women are weeping and wringing their hands
   For those who will never come home to the town ;
For men must work, and women must weep,
And the sooner 'tis over, the sooner to sleep,
     And good-bye to the bar and its moaning.

CHARLES KINGSLEY.

THE SANDS OF DEE.

" O MARY, go and call the cattle home,
    And call the cattle home,
    And call the cattle home,
  Across the sands of Dee ; "
The western wind was wild and dank with foam,
  And all alone went she.

The western tide crept up along the sand,
    And o'er and o'er the sand,
    And round and round the sand,
  As far as eye could see.
The rolling mist came down and hid the land,
  And never home came she.

" O, is it weed, or fish, or floating hair—
    A tress of golden hair,
    A drownèd maiden's hair,
  Above the nets at sea ?
Was never salmon yet that shone so fair
  Among the stakes at Dee."

They rowed her in across the rolling foam,
    The cruel crawling foam,
    The cruel hungry foam,
  To her grave beside the sea :
But still the boatmen hear her call the cattle home
  Across the sands of Dee.

CHARLES KINGSLEY.

     SEA · MUSIC.

SUNDAY—A CALM AT SEA.

Now the wild waters sway themselves to rest,
    Soft, softly kissed,
And like a benediction o'er the sea
    Broods the still mist.

Oh ! Holy Spirit, keep a Sabbath here
    In my wild breast ;
Bending benignant from thy heavenly sphere
    Teach me to rest.

Too late repentant, I've no limpid depth
    Where Thou might'st lie,
Only the welter that the weary waves
    Lift to the sky.

Only myself, of all thy beauteous world
    Nothing is mine,
No deep reflection from beloved lives,
    No light divine.—

Ah ! see that sparkle ; see, the mists uproll
    In noiseless flight !
For me the omen ;—in my eventide
    Shall there be light ?

Hon. Mrs. O. N. Knox.

A SEA-GLIMPSE.

HIGH tide, and the year at the ebb :
  The sea is in a dream to-day :
The sky is a gossamer web
  Of sapphire, and pearl, and gray :

A veil over rock and boat ;
  A breath on the tremulous blue,
Where the dim sails lie afloat,
  Or, unaware, slip from view.

They veer to the rosy ray ;
  They dusk to the violet shade ;
Like a thought they flit away ;
  Like a foolish hope, they fade.

But listen ! a sudden flash !
  A ship is heaving in sight,
With a stir, and a noisy dash
  Of the salt foam, seething white.

Tar-grimed and weather-stained,
  The sailors shout from her deck :
Naught of the sky blue-veined,
  Or the dreamy waves they reck.

And the sunburnt girl, who stands
  Where her feet on the wet wrack slip,—

Eyes shaded with little brown hands,—
She sees but the coming ship.

                    LUCY LARCOM.

THE sea-weed rises, sunset-red,
Its rosy tips to lift and lave,—
Its delicate fronds float all outspread
Upon the tossing of the wave.
The light that leaves the sunset skies
Lingers to kiss it ; and the far
Sea-voices round it surge and rise,
That sound from where old twilights are.

                    M. C. GILLINGTON.

THE deep mid-ocean waters perpetually
Call to the land, and call unanswered still.

                    A. MARY F. ROBINSON.

THE sunlights waver from rock to rock,
    And the pied clouds come and go
And the restless bay, with a flickering mock
    Quivers back shadow and glow.

                    AUGUSTA WEBSTER.

THE wanton water leaps in sport,
And rattles down the pebbly shore.

                    THOMAS LOVELL BEDDOES.

ON THE BEACH IN NOVEMBER.

My heart's Ideal, that somewhere out of sight
  Art beautiful and gracious and alone,—
  Haply, where blue Saronic waves are blown
On shores that keep some touch of old delight,—
How welcome is thy memory, and how bright,
  To one who watches over leagues of stone
  These chilly northern waters creep and moan
From weary morning unto weary night.
O Shade-form, lovelier than the living crowd,
So kind to votaries, yet thyself unvowed,
  So free to human fancies, fancy-free,
  My vagrant thought goes out to thee, to thee,
As wandering lonelier than the Poet's cloud,
  I listen to the wash of this dull sea.

EDWARD CRACROFT LEFROY.

THE PHANTOM SHIP.

WE touch Life's shore as swimmers from a wreck
　　Who shudder at the cheerless land they reach,
　　And find their comrades gathered on the beach
Watching a fading sail, a small white speck—
The Phantom ship, upon whose ample deck
　　There seemed awhile a homeward place for each ;
　　The crowd still wring their hands and still beseech,
But see, it fades, in spite of prayer and beck.

Let those who hope for brighter shores no more
　　Not mourn, but turning inland, bravely seek
What hidden wealth redeems the shapeless shore.
　　The strong must build stout cabins for the weak ;
Must plan and stint ; must sow, and reap and store ;
　　For grain takes root though all seems bare and bleak.

EUGENE LEE-HAMILTON.

SUNKEN GOLD.

In dim green depths rot ingot-laden ships,
  While gold doubloons that from the drowned hand
    fell
  Lie nestled in the ocean-flower's bell
With Love's gemmed rings once kissed by now dead
    lips.
And round some wrought-gold cup the sea-grass whips
  And hides lost pearls, near pearls still in their shell,
  Where sea-weed forests fill each ocean dell,
And seek dim sunlight with their countless tips.

So lie the wasted gifts, the long-lost hopes,
  Beneath the now hushed surface of myself,
In lonelier depths than where the diver gropes.
    They lie deep, deep ; but I at times behold
  In doubtful glimpses, on some reefy shelf,
    The gleam of irrecoverable gold.

Eugene Lee-Hamilton.

SEA-SHELL MURMURS.

THE hollow sea-shell which for years hath stood
  On dusty shelves, when held against the ear
  Proclaims its stormy parent ; and we hear
The faint far murmur of the breaking flood.
We hear the sea.   The sea ?   It is the blood
  In our own veins, impetuous and near,
  And pulses keeping pace with hope and fear
And with our feelings' ever shifting mood.

Lo ! in my heart I hear, as in a shell,
  The murmur of a world beyond the grave,
    Distinct, distinct, though faint and far it be.
Thou fool ; this echo is a cheat as well,—
  The hum of earthly instincts ; and we crave
    A world unreal as the shell-heard sea.

EUGENE LEE-HAMILTON.

THE TIDE RISES, THE TIDE FALLS.

THE tide rises, the tide falls,
The twilight darkens, the curlew calls ;
Along the sea-sands damp and brown
The traveller hastens toward the town,
    And the tide rises, the tide falls.

Darkness settles on roofs and walls,
But the sea in the darkness calls and calls ;
The little waves, with their soft, white hands,
Efface the footprints in the sands,
    And the tide rises, the tide falls.

The morning breaks ; the steeds in their stalls
Stamp and neigh, as the hostler calls ;
The day returns, but never more
Returns the traveller to the shore,
    And the tide rises, the tide falls.

LONGFELLOW.

THE SEA-DIVER.

My way is on the bright blue sea,
    My sleep upon the rocky tide ;
And many an eye has followed me,
    Where billows clasp the worn sea-side.

My plumage bears the crimson blush,
    When ocean by the sun is kissed !
When fades the evening's purple flush,
    My dark wing cleaves the silver mist.

Full many a fathom down beneath
    The bright arch of the splendid deep,
My ear has heard the sea-shell breathe
    O'er living myriads in their sleep.

They rested by the coral throne,
    And by the pearly diadem,
Where the pale sea-grape had o'ergrown
    The glorious dwelling made for them.

At night, upon my storm-drenched wing,
    I poised above a helmless bark,
And soon I saw the shattered thing
    Had passed away and left no mark.

And when the wind and storm had done,
    A ship, that had rode out the gale,

Sunk down without a signal-gun,
　And none was left to tell the tale.

I saw the pomp of day depart—
　The cloud resign its golden crown,
When to the ocean's beating heart
　The sailor's wasted corse went down.

Peace be to those whose graves are made
　Beneath the bright and silver sea !
Peace that their relics there were laid,
　With no vain pride and pageantry.

LONGFELLOW.

THE wave
Drove the pebbles up the beach,
Then resilient to the main
Drew them with it back again.

WILLIAM BELL SCOTT.

TWAS then the moon sailed clear of the rock
　On high in her hollow dome ;
And still as aloft with hoary crest
　Each clamorous wave rang home,
Like fire in snow the moonlight blazed
　Amid the champing foam.

D G. ROSSETTI.

FROM " SEA-WEED."

WHEN descends on the Atlantic
      The gigantic
Storm-wind of the equinox,
Landward in his wrath he scourges
      The toiling surges,
Laden with sea-weed from the rocks :

From Bermuda's reefs ; from the edges
      Of sunken ledges,
In some far-off, bright Azore ;
From Bahama, and the dashing,
      Silver-flashing
Surges of San Salvador ;

From the tumbling surf, that buries
      The Orkneyan skerries,
Answering the hoarse Hebrides ;
And from wrecks of ships, and drifting
      Spars, uplifting
On the desolate, rainy seas ;—

Ever drifting, drifting, drifting,
      On the shifting
Currents of the restless main ;
Till in sheltered coves, and reaches
      Of sandy beaches
All have found repose again.

LONGFELLOW.

THE SOUND OF THE SEA.

THE Sea awoke at midnight from its sleep,
  And round the pebbly beaches far and wide
  I heard the first wave of the rising tide
  Rush onward with uninterrupted sweep ;
A voice out of the silence of the deep,
  A sound mysteriously multiplied
  As of a cataract from the mountain's side,
  Or roar of winds upon a wooded steep.
So comes to us at times, from the unknown
  And inaccessible solitudes of being,
  And rushing of the sea-tides of the soul ;
And inspirations that we deem our own
  Are one divine foreshadowing and foreseeing
  Of things beyond our reason and control.

LONGFELLOW.

THE SECRET OF THE SEA.

AH ! what pleasant visions haunt me
 As I gaze upon the sea !
All the old romantic legends,
 All my dreams, come back to me.

Sails of silk and ropes of sendal,
 Such as gleam in ancient lore ;
And the singing of the sailors,
 And the answer from the shore !

Most of all, the Spanish ballad
 Haunts me oft, and tarries long,
Of the noble Count Arnaldos,
 And the sailor's mystic song.

Like the long waves on a sea-beach,
 Where the sand as silver shines,
With a soft, monotonous cadence
 Flow its unrhymed lyric lines ;—

Telling how the Count Arnaldos,
 With his hawk upon his hand,
Saw a fair and stately galley
 Steering onward to the land ;—

How he heard the ancient helmsman
 Chant a song so wild and clear,

That the sailing sea-bird slowly
   Poised upon the mast to hear.

Till his soul was full of longing,
   And he cried with impulse strong,
" Helmsman ! for the love of heaven,
   Teach me, too, that wondrous song."

" Wouldst thou," so the helmsman answered,
   " Learn the secret of the sea?
Only those who brave its dangers
   Comprehend its mystery !"

In each sail that skims the horizon,
   In each landward-blowing breeze,
I behold that stately galley,
   Hear those mournful melodies ;

Till my soul is full of longing
   For the secret of the sea,
And the heart of the great ocean
   Sends a thrilling pulse throngh me.

                    LONGFELLOW.

       WIDE ocean amorously
Spreads to the sun's embrace ; the dulse-weeds sway,
The glad gulls are afloat.
                E. DOWDEN.

SIR HUMPHREY GILBERT.

Southward with fleet of ice
   Sailed the corsair of Death :
Wild and fast blew the blast,
   And the east wind was his breath.

His lordly ships of ice
   Glistened in the sun ;
On each side, like pennons wide,
   Flashing crystal streamlets run.

His sails of white sea-mist
   Dripped with silver rain ;
But where he passed there were·cast
   Leaden showers o'er the main.

Eastward from Campobello
   Sir Humphrey Gilbert sailed ;
Three days or more seaward he bore,
   Then, alas ! the land-wind failed. .

Alas ! the land-wind failed,
   And ice-cold grew the night :
And never more, on sea or shore,
   Should Sir Humphrey see the light.

He sat upon the deck,
   The Book was in his hand ;

" Do not fear ! Heaven is as near,'
He said, " by water as by land ! "

In the first watch of the night,
  Without a signal's sound,
Out of the sea mysteriously
  The fleet of Death rose all round.

The moon and the evening star
  Were hanging in the shrouds ;
Every mast, as it passed,
  Seemed to rake the passing clouds.

They grappled with their prize,
  At midnight black and cold !
As of a rock was the shock ;
  Heavily the ground-swell rolled.

Southward through day and dark,
  They drift in close embrace,
With mist and rain, to the open main ;
  Yet there seems no change of place.

Southward, for ever southward,
  They drift through dark and day ;
And like a dream, in the Gulf-stream
  Sinking, vanish all away.

LONGFELLOW.

THREE POOR FISHERMEN'S SONG.

WE be three poor fishermen,
  Who daily toil the seas ;
We spend our lives in jeopardy,
  While others live at ease.
The sky looks black around, around,
  The sky looks black around,
And he that would be merry, boys,
  Come haul his boat a-ground

We cast our line along the shore
  In stormy wind and rain ;
And every night we land our nets,
  Till daylight comes again
The sky looks black around, around,
  The sky looks black around,
And he that would be merry, boys,
  Come haul his boat a-ground.

MARK LONSDALE.

CALM and unruffled is the bay,
There is not even a breath at play,
To make a ripple in the sun,
That since the summer day begun
Has shown the Hebridean isles
A cloudless visage, bright with smiles.
On the low rocks that fringe the sea,
The brown dulse welters lazily ;
The sea-gulls, hovering, milky white,
Display their pinions to the light ;
And dart and wheel with sudden cry
Or drop like snow-flakes from the sky.

CHARLES MACKAY.

By the lone sea shore
    Mournfully beat the waves,
Mournfully evermore
    The wild wind sobs and raves.
A sadness and a sense of deep unrest
Brood on the clouds and on the waters' breast.
    But lo ! the white sea-mew careering,
        Floats indolently by,
    And lo ! a snowy sail appearing
        Gleams fair against the sky,
The sadness and the loneliness depart,
And nature smiles with sympathy of heart.

CHARLES MACKAY.

Isle after isle with grey empurpled rocks,
Breasted in steadfast majesty the shocks,
Stupendous, of the wild Atlantic wave ;
Many a desolate sonorous cave
Re-echoed through its inmost vaults profound
The mighty diapason and full sound
Of Corryvreckan—awful orator
Preaching to lonely isles with eloquent roar.

CHARLES MACKAY.

The lonely margin of the sea,
Whose crested waves beat hoarsely on the shore,
Warring against it with perpetual feud.

CHARLES MACKAY.

With a stifled moan
The brooding sea remembered some old grief

WILLIAM SHARP.

The sunrise flashes and floats and flickers red o'er the
      lonely sea ;
The long wet sands bear a red refrain, and the clouds in
      their soft sky home ;
The red cliffs answer the ruddy height, and the hollow of
      lifting waves
Is red with seaweed and rolling sand, and crested with
      rosy foam.

M. C. GILLINGTON.

And downward whirled upon its ocean-bed
  Assails its floods with phosphor-dripping fires.

Nature's imperious passions intertwine,
  And one great spirit moves upon the sea ;
With silver light the emerald waters shine
  Along the procreant path of Deity.

Where the charmed moon a milder day has shed,
  Venus, the love-star, burns : her virgin gifts
From heaven to those blest waters she has sped,
  Wave over wave her paler image drifts.

   *   *   *   *   *   *

And now, lest nature slumber o'er desire,
  The molten passions part, the winds are free,
The sweltered air inflames, the flashing fire
  Darts at the jealous fierce uprising sea.

The curdled foam whitens the watery night,
  Froths up the weeds that, hurried on amain,
Like congregated porpoises in flight,
  Are heaped in shoals upon the furrowed plain.

   *   *   *   *   *   *

A moist, heart-ripening calm has come to rot
  Delved shores, despoiled by the unnatural wave
And swarming with sea monsters ill-begot
  That crawl to perish, lacking all they crave.

Sea-weeds are piled in stacks upon the beach,
  And crisp for fuel for the hungry sun ;

CAUGHT IN THE NETS.

" WOULD I were back, now, in my own sea-caves !
Curse that March twilight, and those stormy waves
Which rioted above me till I said
I too must rise and frolic, so I sped
Up dim green twilights of the under sea ;
And louder seemed the waves to call to me,
Until I dashed their foam apart, and lo !
The sky above with fire seemed to glow,
And in the waste wide glare of crimson light
Made merry the mad waves, all vast and white,
And each to each loud roared some secret thing ;
And the wind seemed a strange new song to sing,
And wantoned with the waves in violent play,
As great sea-monsters do, then fled, and they ;
Roared after, and made haste upon her track back,
Then, suddenly turning, she would hurl them
And they, with their own speed and rage made blind,
Wild, rent, and staggering before that Wind,
Fell, and in falling dashed up high their spray,
As with it they would drown the eyes of day.

" Being of hearing quick, it seemed to me
I heard strange sounds abroad upon the sea,
That cursed March twilight ; yea, but it was fun
To swing in the waves and see the blood-red sun
Strike sharp their white and hurrying heights between,
And when the wind would cut too strong and keen,

N

Just for a moment the waves dive under,
And go, as it were, through the heart of the thunder.

"How sweet the wood smelt, by the wave washed
    warm !
Ah, could I smell it now, and hear the storm
Make white and loud the sea above my head,
I would not leave again my soft sea-bed,
And coral groves the dear sea-girls come through
Singing the songs I love to hearken to.
That last time that I went through a great wave
Something did catch about me ; and some waif
Of monstrous floating weed it was, I thought ;
But when about my head and feet it caught
And seemed to bear me forward, surely then
I knew myself snared in the nets of men—
The nets wherein our simple fish are taken.
Then, with great fear the heart in me was shaken ;
My one hope was, I knew, to break the net.
For this I strove, while, with my face down set,
Through all the interposing sea I prayed
That some bold merman would make haste to aid.
But all were in their homes—none answered me—
Only, at times, most friendly seemed the sea,
When a great wave would with a mighty blow
Send me afield ; but in the fall and flow
I spun round helplessly, half choked and blind,
Hearing above me the singing of the wind.
Then frantically the net I strove to rend,
But, being weak, came suddenly the end—
A strain, a rush, the wind cold on my breast,

No sea, then light—and darkness was the rest,
Until I found myself here, and breast high
In dead sea-water, and above no sky,
Nor light of sea, but something hard and black ;
Ah me ! if I could only once go back !

" I heard a mighty noise about me ; then
I looked into the faces of cursed men.
Right hard they stared. They questioned me, I knew,
But never a word from me their cunning drew.
They gave me food, of which I was full glad,
And strange it was, and sweet, so that I had
Some joy in eating it ; and fish they gave,
Dear fish, that smelt and tasted of the wave ;
And then they left me dark and lonely there.

"There was no sound at all upon the air
The awful silence filled me with such dread
I violently dashed with hands and head
The water round me, that some sound might be,
Some littlest whisper from the far-off sea ;
But with the light of day came sounds again,
And strange it was to me and bitter pain
To hear the wind outside but not the sea.
Then came fresh faces and looked hard at me
In the cold, pitiless glare of the new day.
I heard them say it was the time to pray,
And one man cast a chain my neck about,
And with a mighty grasp he dragged me out,
Right out into the sunlight and the wind,

And some men walked before, and some behind.
So on we wended, till we reached a hall,
Where all around upon their knees did fall,
And made together a most dismal noise.
Then one cried to them, in a louder voice,
Whereat more wail upon the air they poured,
Then rose.   Next in their midst a monster roared,
Whereat they yelled ; yea, all they yelled as one,
So that I thought by fear they were undone ;
And much I marvelled that they kept their ground,
For still that monster made the dreadest sound ;
Then ceased he, and they ceased, and one man rose
And shouted to them, and with many blows
Did beat himself, and long and loud he screamed,
And like some fearful dream that I had dreamed
It seemed to me, and full of dread I was,
Not knowing well what next might come to pass ;
But back they took me to my lonely place,
And here go by the dreary nights and days.

" O shining home wherein are all things fair,
O sea, O world of mine, where art thou, where ?
O deep sea caves, wherein strange, rare things are,
And great sea shells, that praise the sea from far !
Green hills of slippery sea-weed, wet and high,
Where green-haired mermaids love full length to lie,
Their faces in the wet weed buried deep,
Till by their gambols tired, they fall asleep !

" What joy it was to dance among the rocks
And startle, unaware, the mild sea flocks ;

Or, from afar, that low, long sound to hear,
Whereby that cruel whaling-ships are near,
One whale warns all the whale-fields, and all start,
Nor rest until they reach a safer part ;
To see the waves above, now green, now blue,
With light of silver fishes flashing through.

" Here through a chink I see the evening sky ;
Sometimes I think my bar is not so high
But I could overleap it, and be free
And so go forth to seek and find the sea.
Even now the gate stands open which leads out—
I hear no sound of any man about—
Shall I do it ?   Gently !   It is done.
Released I stand.   Ah ! which way shall I run ?
Straight on as well as any.   Swift, my feet !
The sky is full of light, the air is sweet,
Fly fast, my feet, and faster, and more fast,
Until my long lost home be found at last.

" What sound is this ahead ?   O joy of joys !
It is the sea's and my own people's voice.
And as more fast I run, more loud it comes,
Mermaidens call me from their deep sea homes ;
And now upon the verge of my own land,
And yet within this world of men I stand.
A vast and empty place it is—ah me !
But I shall sleep to-night beneath the sea,
And wake to hear the great dear waves wash over,
And some sea-girl shall have me for her lover,

And wind about me with her cold green tresses,
And comfort me with damp and salt caresses.
Oh, world of men, good-bye, I love ye not,
Mine is a wilder and a happier lot ;
White in the moonlight shines the flying foam,
Oh joy ! oh joy ! now I make haste and home."

PHILIP BOURKE MARSTON.

THE sky is harsh and the sea shrewd and salt.

D. G. ROSSETTI.

" EACH wave came on a glittering rippled hill,
And lifting us aloft, showed from its height
The waste of waves, and then to lightless night
Dropped us adown, and much ado had we
To ride unspilt the wallow of the sea."

WILLIAM MORRIS.

THE sea tosses and foams to find
Its way up to the cloud and wind.

RALPH WALDO EMERSON.

To the evening's golden gate
The sea has ebbed, and in the offing lies,
Stirless, his mighty heart without a beat.

E. H. BRODIE

A SONG OF THE STORM.

Across the barren moor
We hear the breakers roar,
See them shine upon the shore ;
  Hear, loud, the sea-gulls cry:
The wind blows loud and shrill,
The sea heaves hill on hill,
Moonlight and tempest fill
  The pure and stormy sky.

'Neath clashing winds of night
The sea revels in its might,
And clear the pale, blown light
  Of driven billows gleams.
O bright, tempestuous sea !
From whose gaping foam-mouths flee
Ships hunted to the lea,
  As souls by evil dreams.

   *   *   *   *   *

Sea-shrieks come loud and long,
Through the thunder and the song
Of breakers white and strong,
  Exploding on the land.
Against the cliffs the wind
Strikes madly, being blind,
What shall the day-break find
  Upon the barren shore.

O white and windy deep,
How many millions sleep
'Neath thy valley and thy steep ;
  O bright careering sea !
O white, warm, bubbling spray,
Blown hissing all one way,—
O loud, resounding bay !
  O lorn and stricken lea !

PHILIP BOURKE MARSTON.

AND like the moan of lions hurt to death
Came the sea's hollow noise along the night.

A. C. SWINBURNE.

THE SOUTH FORELAND.

STORMY SUNSET.

ACROSS th' ensanguined sea the sun
  Sinks slowly through the blood-red west ;
  The wind hath moaned itself to rest ;
A star leaps forth—the day is done ;
Far down beneath the tide doth lift
Itself against the cliff, with swift

Resurge adown the shingly shore,
And hollow, deep, resilient roar.

WILLIAM SHARP.

THE OLD CHURCHYARD OF BONCHURCH.

THE churchyard leans to the sea with its dead—
It leans to the sea with its dead so long.
Do they hear, I wonder, the first bird's song,
When the winter's anger is all but fled,
The high, sweet voice of the west wind,
The fall of the warm, soft rain,
When the second month of the year
Puts heart in the earth again?

Do they hear, through the glad April weather,
The green grasses waving above them?
Do they think there are none left to love them,
They have lain for so long there, together?
Do they hear the note of the cuckoo,
The cry of gulls on the wing,
The laughter of winds and waters,
The feet of the dancing Spring?

Do they feel the old land slipping seaward,
The old land, with its hills and its graves,
As they gradually slide to the waves
With the wind blowing on them from leeward?
Do they know of the change that awaits them,
The sepulchre vast and strange?
Do they long for the days to go over,
And bring that miraculous change?

Or they love, perhaps, their night with no moonlight,
With no starlight, no dawn in its gloom,
And they sigh—" 'Neath the snow, or the bloom
Of the wild things that wave from our night,
We are warm, through winter or summer ;
We hear the winds blow, and say—
' The storm-wind blows over our heads,
But we, here, are out of its way.' "

Do they mumble low, one to another,
With a sense that the waters that thunder
Shall ingather them all, draw them under,
" Ah ! how long to our moving, brother ?
How long shall we quietly rest here,
In graves of darkness and ease ?
The waves, even now, may be on us,
To draw us down under the seas ! "

Do they think 'twill be cold when the waters
That they love not, that neither can love them,
Shall eternally thunder above them ?
Have they dread of the sea's shining daughters,
That people the bright sea-regions
And play with the young sea-kings ?
Have they dread of their cold embraces,
And dread of all strange sea-things ?

But their dread or their joy—it is bootless :
They shall pass from the breast of their mother ;
They shall lie low, dead brother by brother,

In a place that is radiant and fruitless,
And the folk that sail over their heads
In violent weather
Shall come down to them, haply, and all
They shall lie there, together.

PHILIP BOURKE MARSTON.

"HE passed the sea,
And reached a river opening into it
Across the which the white-winged fowl did flit
From cliff to cliff, and on the sandy bar
The fresh waves and the salt waves were at war,
At turning of the tide."

WILLIAM MORRIS.

AND from steep to steep
Of heaven they saw the sweet sheet lightning leap
And laugh its heart out in a thousand smiles,
When the clear sea for miles on glimmering miles
Burned as though dawn were strewn abroad astray,
Or, showering out of heaven, all heaven's array
Had paven instead the waters.

A. C. SWINBURNE.

FROM " MODERN LOVE."

MARK where the pressing wind shoots javelin-like
Its skeleton shadow on the broad-back'd wave !
Here is a fitting spot to dig Love's grave ;
Here where the ponderous breakers plunge and strike,
And dart their hissing tongues far up the sand ;
In hearing of the ocean, and in sight
Of those ribb'd wind-streaks running into white.
If I the death of Love had deeply plann'd,
I never could have made it half so sure,
As by the unbless'd kisses which upbraid
The full-waked sense ; or, failing that, degrade !
'Tis morning : but no morning can restore
What we have forfeited.   I see no sin :
The wrong is mix'd.   In tragic life, God wot,
No villain need be !   Passions spin the plot :
We are betray'd by what is false within.

GEORGE MEREDITH.

AND when the dull sky darkened down to the edges,
And the keen frost kindled in sky and spar,
The sea might be known by a noise on the ledges
Of the lone crags, gathering power from afar
Thro' his roaring bays, and crawling back
Hissing, as o'er the wet pebbles he dragg'd
His skirt of foam, fray'd, dripping, and jagg'd
And reluctantly fell down the smooth hollow shell
O the night.

OWEN MEREDITH.

AND the blear-eyed filmy sea did boom
With his old mysterious hungering sound.

OWEN MEREDITH.

THE Mid Sea that moans with memories.

GEORGE ELIOT.

AND in haste the refluent ocean
Fled away from the shore, and left the line of the sand-
    beach
Covered with waifs of the tide, with kelp and the slip-
    pery sea-weed. . . .
Back to its nethermost caves retreated the bellowing
    ocean,
Dragging adown the beach the rattling pebbles, and
    leaving
Inland and far up the shore the stranded boats of the
    sailors.

LONGFELLOW

SONG.

As the unhastening tide doth roll,
Dear and desired, upon the whole
Long shining strand, and floods the caves,
Your love comes filling with happy waves
The open sea-shore of my soul.

But inland from the seaward spaces,
None knows, not even you, the place
Brimmed at your coming, out of sight
—The little solitudes of delight
This tide constrains in dim embraces.

You see the happy shore, wave-rimmed,
But know not of the quiet dimmed
Rivers your coming floods and fills,
The little pools 'mid happier hills,
My silent rivulets, over-brimmed.

What, I have secrets from you? Yes.
But O my Sea, your love doth press
And reach in further than you know,
And fill all these ; and when you go,
There's loneliness in loneliness.

Alice Meynell

FROM " ANCHORED."

AND suddenly there springs
   Upon the wide sea plain
A breeze like fanning wings,
   And life revives again.
The pearly lines on foam
   Steal onwards, crisp and sweet,
Till to the cliffs they come,
   And eddy at their feet ;
And wavelet on wavelet the tide
Races on through the harbour wide.

And the stranded hulls which lay
   All the long day black and dead,
Swing round to the freshening spray,
   And spread their white wings overhead ;
And the gulls mew their strange sea-song,
   And all sea things that be,
On the hot sand fainting long,
   Revive with the kiss of the sea ;
And a sail comes up, ghostly and white,
To where it shall sojourn to-night.

LEWIS MORRIS.

FROM "THE DOOM OF KING ACRISIUS."

Now underneath the scarped cliffs of the bay
From horn to horn a belt of sand there lay
Fast lessening as the flood-tide swallowed it,
There all about did the sea-swallows flit,
And from the black rocks yellow hawks flew down,
And cormorants fished amidst the sea-weed brown,
Or on the low rocks nigh unto the sea,
While over all the fresh wind merrily
Blew from the sea, and o'er the pale blue sky
Thin clouds were stretched the way the wind went by,
And forward did the mighty waters press
As though they loved the green earth's steadfastness.

WILLIAM MORRIS.

FROM "OGIER THE DANE."

THE sun is setting in the west, the sky
Is clear and hard, and no clouds come anigh
The golden orb, but further off they lie,
Steel grey and black with edges red as blood,
And underneath them is the weltering flood
Of some huge sea, whose tumbling hills, as they
Turn restless sides about, are black or grey,
Or green, or glittering with the golden flame ;
The wind has fallen now, but still the same
The mighty army moves, as if to drown
This lone, bare rock, whose sheer scarped sides of
　　brown
Cast off the weight of waves in clouds of spray.

WILLIAM MORRIS.

FROM " THE WANDERERS."

SOMETIMES when at night
Beneath the moon I watched the foam fly white
From off our bows, and thought how weak and small
Showed the *Rose-Garland's* mast that looked so tall
Beside the quays of Bremen ; when I saw   .
With measured steps the watch on toward me draw,
And in the moon the helmsman's peering face,
And 'twixt the cordage strained across my place
Beheld the white sail of the *Fighting Man*
Lead down the pathway of the moonlight wan—
Then when the ocean seemed so measureless
The very sky itself might well be less,
When midst the changeless piping of the wind,
The intertwined slow waves pressed on behind
Rolled o'er our wake and made it nought again,
Then would it seem an ill thing and a vain
To leave the hopeful world that we had known,
When all was o'er, hopeless to die alone
Within this changeless world of waters grey.

*   *   *   *   *   *

But this our ease at last a tempest broke
And we must scud before it helplessly,
Fearing each moment lest some climbing sea
Should topple o'er our poop and end us there,
Nathless we 'scaped, and still the wind blew fair
For what we deemed was our right course ; but when
On the third eve, we, as delivered men,

O

Took breath because the gale was now blown out,
And from our rolling neck we looked about
Over the ridges of the dark grey seas,
And saw the sun, setting in golden ease,
Smile out at last from out the just-cleared sky
Over the ocean's weltering misery,
Still nothing of the *Fighting Man* we saw,
Which last was seen when the first gusty flaw
Smote them and us ; but nothing would avail
To mend the thing, so onward we did sail,
But slowly, through the moonlit night and fair,
With all sails set that we could hoist in air,
And rolling heavily at first, for still
Each wave came on a glittering rippled hill,
And lifting us aloft, showed from its height
The waste of waves, and then to lightless night
Dropped us adown, and much ado had we
To ride unsplit the wallow of the sea.

WILLIAM MORRIS.

THE sea
Was filled with light ; in clear blue caverns curled
The breakers, and they ran, and seemed to romp,
As playing at some rough and dangerous game,
While all the nearer waves rushed in to help,
And all the farther heaved their heads to peep,
And tossed the fishing boats.

JEAN INGELOW.

FROM "WIDE IS THE SEA."

WIDE is the sea,
O sailor,—forget it not !
The sea is hollow and wide,
And in its awful deeps abide
Protean forms
Of thousand hoary storms,
That lurk and hide
On crags of sea-worn hills.
There the gnarled monsters never sleep,
But their watch keep,
When the taut canvas fills,
And the beautiful lip
Of the glorious ship,
Amorous, touches the outer deep ;
Then, under the sea,
The word goes round,
And through the white foam-wreath
You see their snarling teeth ;
The small waves creep
Along the ocean breast ;
Winds rise and leap
From crest to crest ;
Then, bounding forth, they fly—
Those monsters—with a dreadful sound,
Clearer and nearer,
Nearer and clearer,
Until they bound

        Over hull and deck
        Mast-high,
        And all the multitudinous cry
        Of the wild hell-dogs bursts
        Over a wreck.

                            JAMES H. MORSE.

        As his who on some midnight hears
    Upon a close, and yet night-hidden strand,
    The roused sea calling to the silent land,
    The strong sea stricken of the storm wind's hand ;
        And as he listens, feels himself the pain
        Of shipwrecked men, who battle with the main.

                            PHILIP B. MARSTON.

    AND shining with a gloom, the water grey
        Swang in its moon-taught way.

                    ELIZABETH BARRETT BROWNING.

    BEAUTIFUL, beautiful the Mother lay,
    Crownèd with silver spray,
    The greenness gathering trustfully around
        The peace of her great heart, while on her breast
    The wayward Waters, with a weeping sound,
        Were sobbing into rest.

                        ROBERT BUCHANAN.

ALONG THIS FRONT.

I.

ALONG this front of hoary pines
  I listen to the sea ;
Betwixt two realms whose long confines
  Wage war eternally.

I see the marshalled billows drive
  With might against the coast ;
I see the hills thrust back and rive
  The long, embattled host ;

And twice betwixt the morn and morn,
  Who stands upon this lea
May see the might that comes in scorn,
  Rolled back in agony.

So too, year-long, yon idle vane,
  That lives for that alone,
Reports along a windy main
  A conflict here unknown.

And who shall tell the ebb and flow
  Among the silent stars,
Whose tides unseen sweep to and fro
  In their eternal wars ?

Within my soul, too, a dim coast,
  Whereon I seem to hear

The thunder of a hostile host
   Recede and then draw near,—

Two mighty powers, whose endless strife
   'Tis mine alone to know ;
And, though they tear me limb and life,
   I watch them down below ;—

Still watch, and little power to give
   To either part have I,—
With this to win the fight and live,
   With that to lose and die.

JAMES H. MORSE.

NOT where they clash ashore, and break and moan,
Are waters deadliest.

A MARY F. ROBINSON.

ALL still, all silent, save the sobbing rush
Of rippling waves, that lapsed in silver hush
Upon the beach.

ADELAIDE ANNE PROCTER.

LISTENING now to the tide in its broad-flung ship-wreck-
   ing roar,
Now to the scream of a madden'd beach dragg'd down by
   the wave.

LORD TENNYSON.

ALONE BY THE BAY.

HE is gone.　O my heart, he is gone ;
　And the sea remains and the sky,
And the skiffs flit in and out,
　And the white-winged yachts go by.

The waves run purple and green,
　And the sunshine glints and glows,
And freshly across the bay
　The breath of the morning blows.

I liked it better last night,
　When the dark shut down on the main,
And the phantom fleet lay still,
　And I heard the waves complain.

For the sadness that dwells in my heart,
　And the rune of their endless woe,—
Their longing and void despair,—
　Kept time in their ebb and flow.

LOUISE CHANDLER MOULTON.

HIGH TIDE AT MIDNIGHT.

No breath is on the glimmering ocean floor,
   No blast beneath the windless Pleiades,
But thro' dead night a melancholy roar,
   A voice of moving and of marching seas,—
The boom of thundering waters on the shore
   Sworn with slow force by desolate degrees
Once to go on, and whelm for evermore
   Earth and her folk and all their phantasies.
Then half asleep in the great sound I seem
Lost in the starlight, dying in a dream
   Where overmastering Powers abolish me,—
Drown, and thro' dim euthanasy redeem
My merged life in the living ocean-stream
   And soul-environing of shadowy sea.

Frederick W. H. Myers.

A SEA SYMPHONY.

I.

TEMPEST.

OCEAN, eternal mother of the free !
Thine uproar is the sound of Liberty.
Shout forth a clarion-call tempestuously !
" England, though comfortable sleep be sweet,
Whispering emperors ominously meet :
What if they murder Freedom, murder man ?
Shall not thy rent red flag inflame the van
Of battle as erst?   Arouse thee unto war !
Hearken how thunderpeals from Trafalgar,
Nile, and the Baltic, thine heroic past,
Fill loud my clarions of surge and blast !
Awake ! for fear thy lethargy may prove the last ! "
Grand lion-leap of billows ! how they fall,
Plunging with hunger to devour the shore !
Hurled mountain of blown billow thwart the wall
Of cliff precipitous bursting with stupendous roar !
Cavernous halls of hoary mountains under
Shake with a shock of subterranean thunder,
Rumble with roll of long reverberate thunder !
Crushed all the turbid water-mountain toils
Whose slain, immense, pale, shadowy ghost is thrown
High among hurrying storm-cloud, and recoils
Seethingly, limply plashing on the stone.
While underneath a baffled field of foam,

Poured out disorderly, retreats to rise
One fulvous mass of spume upon a dome
Of wave colossal threatening the skies :
Lo ! as it sweeps imperial, the curl
In toppling hangs arrested by a swirl
Refluent baffled ; rears aloft to hurl
All, one grim rampart perpendicular,
Bodily heavenward, whose wrestling froth,
In terrible welter of tumultuous wrath,
Flickers to momentary crags of spar ;
Headlong to ruin charges with an ocean jar,
A headlong ruin of water, heard inland afar !
Terrific hurricane of howling wind and sea !
Cower from the whirlwind lest in scorn it scatter thee !
Or fling thee in the ravening cauldron there—
Cling to the rock—let tawny salt sea foam flakes tear
Hissingly o'er thee from a turbulent despair !
Shout forth thy drowned and feeble human shout of joy,
In fellow-feeling with the elements, a toy
Of the blind Titans, yet a toy that knows. .   .   .
.   .   .   .   But what is this at hand that reels, and drifts,
        and bows?
Not helpless chaos of a huge oarweed,
Torn up and strewn far, senseless rage to feed—
A ship ! a ship ! a horrible vision here !
One snapt mast with its tangling cordage-gear
Overboard flounders ; on the flooded deck
Three scared men desperate clinging strain the neck
To look for any help toward the rocky roar ;
Whom Death alone confronts upon the awful shore !
A small black dog i' the hatchway yelping piteously—
I see it still—a crash—anon victoriously
Climb maniac cataracts upon rent planks and corpses
        clamorously !

II.

CALM.

AFTER two days I lay reclined in peace
Near the sea margin; delicate soft fleece
Of cloud lay poised above me, and the sea
Slumbered about her shores, how tranquilly !
Gentle as a child she opened her blue eyes
In murmurous foamsmile of a faint surprise,
Touching the strand : yon vaporous headlands are
Suffused with mellow sunlight, while afar
A nebulous isle half fades into the sky,
Like some dear hoped-for possibility.
Hushful sea-murmur lulls all pain to sleep,
Breathing enchantment from the Holy Deep—
One feels so happy here, one fain would weep !
Among fair silver labryinths a stain
Of solemn purple on the lonely main
Long from one cloud lies ; in still mother o' pearl
Yonder no white sail will a vessel furl
To-day, among "the innumerable smile "
Of one who hides no wrath, nor harbours guile ;
Zephyr with his soft seaplume fans the while.
Quietly wander by the quiet shore,
To find enrapturing wonders more and more !
Here ankle-deep in valvéd shelly shingle,
Merry young children, with white limbs atingle,
Leap laughing, while a playful ripple blue
Merrily laves them ; ah ! how fair the hue
Of azure sea set by a dovelike tone

Of boulders, where I wander all alone !
Now and then their prevailing hue will bring
Aerial colour, soft as seamew wing,
On water, modulating mirrored sky
To fill my pureness of chalcedony.
In still sea-waters of a cove will grow
Slim growths of plashing crystal, when there flow
Oceanward tinkling, rillets from above,
Born among hazels, while with ocean love
Glisten low-lying rocks in many a cove.
Weird block of waveworn labyrinthine grey
Hollowed out, with small opening for day
Somewhere concealed as one explores, a fairy
Or mermaiden may haunt thee, little wary
Of man's intrusion on her lonely spot,
Or sleepy seal may use thee, twilit grot.
But many a wondrous cavern richly hued
Quavers in delicate waterlight, imbued
Their dim recesses with a dusk maroon,
Mossgreen or lilac, all a quiet tune
Of heaving water hearing, while sea-flowers
Crimson or wavegreen bud in all the bowers.
This lofty cave's a gorgeous palace-gate,
Where some Sea-Genius holds royal state :
Surely the stillness may invite to float
Pensively hither in a slender boat,
And pore upon the faint seagroves remote !
Where now thy terrible moods, O sea ? .   .   .
                              .   .   .   .   But this ?
In yon dark fissure where an ocean-kiss
Tenderly falls in music, a dim mass
Sways with nigh impalpably-heaved glass :
Creep near . . . it wears a horrible human shape !
An eyeless head is nodding from the nape.

Poor ghastly mockery of a human form,
Jammed here in fierce delirium of storm !
And look ! a shadowy monster in the deep
Looms huge and hungry near the awful sleep !
Yonder a board swims rusty-nailed and rent,
Four painted letters with the tangle blent.
There is a mellow dark-eyed maid in Spain,
Who waits a token from a foreign main.

III.

TWILIGHT.

A LITTLE wandering child has lost his way
On a hushed mountain at the close of day,
On a brine-bitten waste that slopes to grey
Abrupt cliffs, where a melancholy sea
Expands afar, slow-wrinkling mercury :
One cold, dim gleam, with three dark shadows vast,
From clouds immense in faded blues amassed,
Shadows that in a dreary twilight brood
Portentous phantom Presences, imbued,
Silently awful with a life not ours ;
While on the sea-shore formidably lowers
A corrugated monster bulk of stone ;
Some huge unwieldy monster left alone,
Slumbrous aware, with face toward old Ocean,
Since some pre-human age when such as he had motion.

Rude, samphired, pinnacled, great crags arise
Sheer from dull seas into low, dusky skies ;
And one, a ghostly giant, leans athwart

Twilight, to watch him wandering, huge and swart !
Through one wild arch in yonder cape wave-worn
Expands a dreary infinite forlorn.
Infinite, pale, and dim and desolate,
Monotonous Ocean, with the Voice of Fate
Breathes homeless, helpless, and disconsolate.
Some sere, sparse mountain-bents moan shivering,
As the gust wearies them, and withered ling.
Near a path, pale with night that deepens round,
A ruinous gate stirs with an eerie sound.
Ah ! were it she who came to seek the child.
His mother ! with a piteous gesture wild
He turns and calls : alas ! she will not come ;
Dead mother knows not he is lost from home !
Dusk flaps a heavy-flighted cormorant,
Whereat the timorous breast begins to pant :
What dwarfed old man distorted threatens him ?
'Tis but a dry tree with blast-writhen limb !
Now, chill at heart, the little wanderer weeps,
And stumbles pale among the rugged steeps.

But God hath pity on a babe's despair :
For now he gains a summit ; unaware
There breaks upon his poor, tear-misted sight
A blissful vision of supreme delight !
Cheery near lights of houses in the town ;
And cheery murmuring human tones are blown
Upon the wind towards him ! then the child
Thanked God who led him hither from the wild ;
Brushed with his hand the tears, and ran so fast,
Clasped in his father's happy arms at last !

IV.

BREEZE.

CLIMB upon yonder ivied neck of rock,
Flanked with twin chasms, and hear unrestful shock
Of tidal water in the caves rebuffed,
With fierce, impatient contumely cuffed,
Along the front of stern embattled coast,
Spat forth in spray from sombre innermost
Hollows; and ever heaving blindly under,
Blundering in with subterranean thunder !
Stumbling and fumbling, water in the caves,
Like a strange, sullen beast, assaults and braves
The rocky scorn for ever ; chafed to froth,
Bellowing snorts in impotent dull wrath ;
So famished beast prowls ever, thrusting snout
Under his bars, in pain till he break out.
Yea, this immortal, subtle, importunate Sea,
Conquers our stolid Earth implacably.
Though round our ruined shores He laugh and dally,
Chafing for war his proud battalions rally.
See how the simmering wash of swelling wave
Feels all alive along rich ooze of cave !
Yon grand expansive green hath belts to-day
Of blue and tawny, flecked with sparkling spray
By the brisk breeze that blows with cheerful play,
Wafting a merry crest in snowy smoke,
Glassed in the billow while it tossed and broke !
And there is evermore a restless wreath
Around the innumerable sharp shark's teeth,
Black flames rough crusted, threatening fangs of
   death.

Yonder, lo ! the tide is flowing ;
Clamber, while the breeze is blowing,
Down to where a soft foam flusters
Dulse and fairy feathery clusters !
While it fills the shelly hollows,
A swift sister billow follows,
Leaps in hurrying with the tide,
Seems the lingering wave to chide ;
Both push on with eager life,
And a gurgling show of strife.
O the salt, refreshing air
Shrilly blowing in the hair !
A keen, healthful savour haunts
Sea-shell, sea-flower, and sea-plants.
Innocent billows on the strand
Leave a crystal over sand
Whose thin ebbing soon is crossed
Of a crystal foam-enmossed,
Variegating silvergrey
Shell-empetalled sand in play :
When from sand dries off the brine,
Vanishes swift shadow fine ;
But a wet sand is a glass
Where the plumy cloudlets pass,
Floating islands of the blue,
Tender, shining, fair and true.

Who would linger idle,
Dallying would lie,
When wind and wave, a bridal
Celebrating, fly ?
Let him plunge among them,
Who hath wooed enough,

Flirted with them, sung them !
In the salt sea-trough
He may win them, onward
On a buoyant crest,
Far to seaward, sunward,
Oceanborne to rest !
Wild wind will sing over him,
And the free foam cover him,
Swimming seaward, sunward,
On a blythe sea-breast !
On a blythe sea-bosom
Swims another too,
Swims a live sea-blossom,
A grey-winged sea-mew.
Grape-green all the waves are
By whose hurrying line
Half of ships and caves are
Buried under brine ;
Supple, shifting ranges
Lucent at the crest
With pearly surface-changes
Never laid to rest :
Now a dipping gunwale
Momently he sees,
Now a fuming funnel,
Or red flag in the breeze.
Arms flung open wide,
Lip the laughing sea ;
For playfellow, for bride,
Claim her impetuously !
Triumphantly exalt with all the free,
Buoyant, bounding splendour of the sea !
And if while on the billow
Wearily he lay,

His awful wild playfellow
Filled his mouth with spray,
Reft him of his breath,
To some far realms away
He would float with Death ;
Wild wind would sing over him,
And the free foam cover him,
Waft him sleeping onward,
Floating seaward, sunward,
All alone with Death ;
In a realm of wondrous dreams,
And shadow-haunted gleams !

HON. RODEN NOEL.

AND while the wind began to sweep
 A music out of sheet and shroud,
 We steered her toward a crimson cloud
That landlike slept along the deep.

LORD TENNYSON.

WITH chafe and change of surges chiming,
 The clashing channels rocked and rang
Large music, wave to wild wave timing,
 And all the choral water sang.

A. C. SWINBURNE.

ALL round the sea wet shining nets were spread,
 Gold shone the cliffs, and all the sea was bright
As through its glowing depths the sun had shed
 His soul in one great ecstasy of light.

PHILIP B. MARSTON.

FROM "TAMERTON CHURCH TOWER.

THE storm at last is come !
Above us, heated fields of mist
    Precipitated cloud.
For shore we pull'd ; the swift keel hiss'd ;
    Above us flew the shroud.
The pale gull flapp'd the stagnant.air ;
    The thunder-drops fell straight.

    *   *   *   *   *

Across the mighty mirror crept,
    In dark'ning blasts the squall;
And round our terror lightly leapt
    Mad wavelets, many and small.
The oars cast by, convuls'd outflew
    Our perilous hope the sail.
None spoke ; all watch'd the waves, that grew
    Under the splashing hail.
With urgent hearts and useless hands,
    We sate and saw them rise,
Coursing to shore in gloomy bands,
    Below the appalling skies.
The wrathful thunder scared the deeps,
    And where, upon our wake,
The sea got up in ghastly heaps,
    White lines of lightning strake.
On, on, with fainting hope we fled,
    Hard-hunted by the grave ;
Slow seem'd it, though like wind we sped
    Over the shouldering wave ;

In front swift rose the crags, where still
　　A storm of sunshine pour'd ;
At last, beneath the southern hill,
　　The pitiless breakers roared.

*　　　*　　　*　　　*　　　*

The billows like some guilty crew
　　Devour'd by vain remorse
Dash'd up the beach, sighing withdrew
　　And mix'd, with murmurs hoarse.

COVENTRY PATMORE.

SORROWFUL surges wailing up the shore.

M. C. GILLINGTON.

THE level sands and grey,
　　Stretch leagues and leagues away,
Down to the border line of sky and foam,
　　A spark of sunset burns,
　　The grey tide-water turns
Back, like a ghost from her forbidden home.

ANDREW LANG.

LIKE one vast sapphire flashing light
The sea, just breathing, shone.

GERALD MASSEY.

THE SECRET OF THE SEA.

WHO knows the mighty secret,
The secret of the sea ?
I love its beauty passing well,
I love the thunder of its swell,
I love the glory of its play,
The glitter of its feathery spray,
But its secret is hid from me.

Who knows the mighty secret—
Who gives the sea its power?
Its laugh will chime with gayest mood,
It gives the friend to solitude ;
It frets with the fretted heart or head,
It mourns the past, it wails the dead,
It lulls the dreamy hour.

Who has the mighty secret?
Never a mortal knows.
By the shells alone is the riddle read,
As they lie deep down in their coral bed
In the depths of the seaweed forest brown,
Where the August sunshine quivers down,
And the great tide comes and goes.

They know the mighty secret ;
They are cast upon the sand ;

We gather them up from the creamy foam,
We bear them away to our island home,
As relics of happy seaside days,
We bear them to dwell where the soft breeze plays
Over the flowery land.

They know the mighty secret ;
They murmur it all day long.
With a passionate wail, with a yearning cry
For the shadowy reef where the surf beats high,
Where the great waves roll for ever and aye,
And their roar swells up to the hanging sky,
And the wind blows wild and strong.

They know the mighty secret ;
We hold them to our ear,
We hear the mystical sound again,
We hear the voice of the restless main,
We know the long monotonous roar,
As the billows break on the rugged shore ;
But that is all we hear.

We cannot read the secret,
We cannot find the key,
Ah ! sully not by earthly guess
Its grandeur and its loveliness ;
Take the infinite gladness of the main,
And fling the poor shell back again,
Back to its parent sea.

SUSAN K. PHILLIPS.

TO A WAVE.

LUCENT wave,
Flash in sparkling bells
On the colour'd stones and tiny shells ;
With low music lave
Shelving rock,
Flood the glassy pool,
Sway the foliage 'neath its crystal cool,
Wake with gentle shock
The anemone,
That, like some lovely flower,
Petals opening 'neath the sunlight's power,
Its beauty spreads to thee.
Let thy salt
To the star-fish bring
Dreams of new and joyous wandering,
In the sea's green vault.
From afar
Cam'st thou slowly on,
Born of breeze that long ago is gone
O'er the sandy bar.
Like a smile
One of thousands fair,
That old ocean's face to-day will wear,
Thou for many a mile,
'Neath the sky,
Wind and slanting light
Sportedst 'mid thy fellows emerald-bright,

Foam-fleck'd glancing by.
O'er thy breast,
Like a thing of snow
Wild the sea-bird flew, and stooping low,
Found thy heaving rest.
So at last,
Joyous still with play,
Towards the shore thou stealest fring'd with spray,
All thyself to cast.
Flashing near,
Spill thy little life,
Death to thee with tender peace seems rife ;
Then wherefore need we fear?

J. PIERCE.

THE slack waves rippling at the smooth flat keel.

J. A. SYMONDS.

As ocean murmurs when the storm is past
And keeps the echoed thunders many days.

ROBERT BUCHANAN.

A GLORIOUS headland bare to sun and sky,
And bleached with all the winds of heaven that be
Winged with the briny odours of the sea.

E. H. BRODIE.

THE TIDE COMING IN.

THE busy waters multitudinous
Lip the dry beach, and, rippling every pool,
Embathe the limpets in their swirlings cool,
And plash upon the rocks, returning thus
To their old haunts, with pleasure tremulous.
The sun just risen gladdens, yet seems to rule
The thronging floods.   How grand their voices, full
Of a strange rapture which, alas ! to us
Is half unknown ; we can but fear and wonder.
And now the breeze is waken'd, furrowing fair
The foam-tipp'd hillocks green that dip asunder,
And with a gentle crash fall here and there,
In creamy plots.   Anon, with voice of thunder,
Old ocean doth his solemn joy declare.

J. PIERCE.

THE CITY IN THE SEA.

Lo ! Death has reared himself a throne
In a strange city lying alone
Far down within the dim West,
Where the good and the bad and the worst and
   the best
Have gone to their eternal rest.
There shrines and palaces and towers—
Time-eaten towers that tremble not—
Resemble nothing that is ours.
Around, by lifting winds forgot,
Resignedly beneath the sky
The melancholy waters lie.

No rays from the holy heaven come down
On the long night-time of that town ;
But light from out the lurid sea
Streams up the turrets silently—
Gleams up the pinnacles far and free—
Up domes—up spires—up kingly halls—
Up fanes—up Babylon-like walls—
Up shadowy long-forgotten bowers
Of sculptured ivy and stone flowers—
Up many and many a marvellous shrine
Whose wreathèd friezes intertwine
The viol, the violet, and the vine,
Resignedly beneath the sky
The melancholy waters lie.

So blend the turrets and shadows there
That all seem pendulous in air,
While from a proud tower in the town
Death looks gigantically down.

There open fanes and gaping graves
Yawn level with the luminous waves.
But not the riches there that lie
In each idol's diamond eye—
Not the gaily-jewelled dead—
Tempt the waters from their bed ;
For no ripples curl, alas !
Along that wilderness of glass—
No swellings tell that winds may be
Upon some far-off happier sea—
No heavings hint that winds have been
On seas less hideously serene.

But lo, a stir is in the air !
The wave—there is a movement there !
As if the towers had thrust aside,
In slightly sinking, the dull tide—
As if their tops had feebly given
A void within the filmy heaven.
The waves have now a redder glow—
The hours are breathing faint and low—
And when, amid no earthly moans,
Down, down that town shall settle hence,
Hell, rising from a thousand thrones
Shall do it reverence.

EDGAR ALLAN POE

OCEAN, THE CAPTIVE.

MEN call thee free, and I have heard the wind
Pass landward, breathed of liberty and thee,
Have watched thy white-maned horses prancing free,
As if their courses could not be confined :
But deeper than the hand of man has mined
Are set the bolts of thy captivity ;
From higher than the eyes of man can see,
The jealous moon thy limbs doth strangely bind.
Thou moanest, " I that am the heaven's own child,
Why, laid within the cruel, cradling shores,
Should I but grow to feel a prisoner's pains ? "
And, like a giant fretting in his chains,
Thou thunderest at Earth's never-yielding doors,
Untamed and tameless and unreconciled.

H. D. RAWNSLEY.

DEEP-SEA CALM.

With what deep calm, and passionlessly great,
Thy central soul is stored, the Equinox
Roars, and the north wind drives ashore his flocks,
Thou heedest not, thou dost not feel the weight
Of the Leviathan, the ships in state
Plough on, and hull with hull in battle shocks,
Unshaken thou ; the trembling planet rocks,
Yet thy deep heart will scarcely palpitate.
Peace-girdle of the world, thy face is moved,
And now thy furrowed brow with fierce light gleams,
Now laughter ripples forth a thousand miles,
But still the calm of thine abysmal streams
Flows round the people of our fretful isles,
And Earth's inconstant fever is reproved.

H. D. RAWNSLEY.

THE GLADNESS OF THE SEA.

LEAGUE after league of sunshine, and a face
As changeful as a lover's, in what love
The sea for tryst comes dancing up the cove;
How light of heart, with what excess of grace,
Does wave on wave its brother shoreward race!
Thrice happy ocean, where thy waters move
Is health, and life, and hope for keels that rove,
Thou bearest home brave ships in thine embrace,
Thou seem'st to hold thy breath, then, laughing, roll
Up the long beach in roar of merriment,
And while the dolphins sport in happy shoal
Far seaward, and glad cries of children sent
Ring from the shore, thy tide has touched my soul,
And I am glad with thy deep-drawn content.

H. D. RAWNSLEY.

ESKMEALS.

OH, joy, where sea and river waters meet,
To watch how swift the wading dotterels ply
Their rosy stilts in pools of bluest sky,
To hear cool sprinklings from their dainty feet !
To lean and listen to the flutings sweet
Of sandpiper, or sad-voiced plover's cry ;
While the grave heron at his fishery
Gleams like a silver sickle through the heat !
Blest be the tide that bared these tawny shelves,
For such a world of food and innocent play !
Man, weary man, with sorrow digs and delves,
But is not glad in winning bread, as they,
Who wait on God, and, careless of themselves,
Take that which Nature else had thrown away.

H. D. RAWNSLEY.

TIDES.

THROUGH the still dusk how sighs the ebb-tide out,
    Reluctant for the reed-beds ! Down the sands
    It washes.   Hark ! Beyond the wan gray strand's
Low limits how the winding channels grieve,
Aware the evasive waters soon will leave
    Them void amid the waste of desolate lands,
    Where shadowless to the sky the marsh expands,
And the noon-heats must scar them, and the drought.

Yet soon for them the solacing tide returns
    To quench their thirst of longing.   Ah, not so
        Works the stern law our tides of life obey !
        Ebbing in the night watches swift away,
    Scarce known ere fled for ever is the flow ;
And in parched channel still the shrunk stream mourns.

                            CHARLES G. D. ROBERTS.

A VISION OF STORM.

A SPOIL-STROWN seaboard desolate,
  With wrack of ruined armaments,
Sand heaped like heroes' graves, and great
  Grey rocks uncouthly poised awry ;
  Stones from the sling of angels hurl'd
That, missing Hell, fell here to lie
  Unrecorded monuments
    Of a forgotten world.

A Titan-woman stoops and graves
  A limit to the weary waves
That hang about, creep in and out
  Her bare white feet, like sickly snakes,
  And rust the chain that binds and breaks
The four winds crouching there her slaves.
  The sea-surf lies in reddened shrouds
Below, above her dusk hair makes
  Gloom as if gather'd tempest clouds.
    In her eyes that never weep
    Lightnings are laid asleep.

A. MARY F. ROBINSON.

FROM "STORNELLI AND STRAMBOTTI."

" As beats the sea against the rocks ! " you cried,
" Against your stubborn will my soul is hurl'd."
You meant the seeming-daunted broken tide,
With scattered spray and shattered crests uncurl'd,
That, from the shore, we pity or deride :
And yet these dying waters, spent and swirl'd,
Their stony limits do themselves decide,
And fashion to their will the unconscious world.

A. MARY F. ROBINSON.

YEA, surely the sea like a harper laid hand on the
        shore as a lyre.

A. C. SWINBURNE.

As on a dull day in an ocean cave
The blind wave feeling round his long sea-hall
In silence.

LORD TENNYSON.

THE sea swept in with moan and foam
        Quickening the stretch of sand.

CHRISTINA ROSSETTI.

FROM "SEA PICTURES."

TWILIGHT.—NORMANDY.

LATE even now, and overclouded skies,
To-night we shall not see the young moon rise ;
The twilight grows, away on either hand
The cliffs are lost in mystic shadowland.
Only low sound of breakers as they die,—
Pale shimmer of waters, and a pale still sky,
Where darkness gathers on the moving sea,
And yet the child laughs light of heart with me,
Still deeper now ;—one little brown-sailed bark
Glides past us seaward drifting into dark ;
The only light is on the white sea-foam,
And the lamp by the crucifix :—come home !

RENNELL RODD.

BY THE SEA.

WHY does the sea moan evermore?
  Shut out from heaven it makes its moan,
It frets against the boundary shore;
  All earth's full rivers cannot fill
  The sea, that drinking thirsteth still.

Sheer miracles of loveliness
  Lie hid in its unlooked-on bed;
Anemones, salt, passionless,
  Blow flower-like; just enough alive
  To blow and multiply and thrive.

Shells quaint with curve, or spot, or spike,
  Encrusted live things argus-eyed,
All fair alike, yet all unlike,
  Are born without a pang, and die
  Without a pang, and so pass by.

CHRISTINA ROSSETTI.

THE SEA-LIMITS.

CONSIDER the sea's listless chime :
   Time's self it is, made audible,—
   The murmur of the earth's own shell.
Secret continuance sublime
   Is the sea's end : our sight may pass
   No furlong further.   Since time was,
This sound hath told the lapse of time.

No quiet, which is death's—it hath
   The mournfulness of ancient life,
   Enduring always at dull strife.
As the world's heart of rest and wrath,
   Its painful pulse is in the sands.
   Last utterly, the whole sky stands,
Grey and not known, along its path.

Listen alone beside the sea,
   Listen alone among the woods ;
   Those voices of twin solitudes
Shall have one sound alike to thee :
   Hark where the murmurs of thronged men
   Surge and sink back and surge again,—
Still the one voice of wave and tree.

Gather a shell from the strown beach
   And listen at its lips : they sigh
   The same desire and mystery,

The echo of the whole sea's speech,
  And all mankind is thus at heart
  . Not anything but what thou art :
And Earth, Sea, Man, are all in each.

DANTE GABRIEL ROSSETTI.

FROM "SOOTHSAY."

THE wild waifs cast up by the sea
Are diverse ever seasonably.
Even so the soul-tides still may land
A different drift upon the sand.
But one the sea is evermore :
And one be still, 'twixt shore and shore,
As the sea's life, thy soul in thee.

DANTE GABRIEL ROSSETTI.

NAY, come up hither.   From this waved-washed mound
  Unto the furthest flood-brim look with me ;
Then reach on with thy thought till it be drown'd.
  Miles and miles distant though the last line be,
And though thy soul sail leagues and leagues beyond,—
  Still, leagues beyond those leagues, there is more sea.

DANTE GABRIEL ROSSETTI.

A SEA-SPELL.

(FOR A PICTURE.)

HER lute hangs shadowed in the apple-tree,
While flashing fingers weave the sweet-strung spell
Between its chords; and as the wild notes swell,
The sea-bird for those branches leaves the sea.
But to what sound her listening ear stoops she?
What netherworld gulf-whispers doth she hear,
In answering echoes from what planisphere,
Along the wind, along the estuary?

She sinks into her spell: and when full soon
Her lips move and she soars into her song,
What creatures of the midmost main shall throng
In furrowed surf-clouds to the summoning rune:
Till he, the fated mariner, hears her cry,
And up her rock, bare-breasted, comes to die?

DANTE GABRIEL ROSSETTI.

AT SEA.

Now the tide is safe and high,
   In the fresh'ning morning breeze,
Over the harbour bar we hie
   Out into the open seas.

With these fisher lads so strong
   And knowing in the water ways,
I'll try to make a summer song,
   The fisher's summer life to praise.

It seems to me the rounded sea
   Begins to swell above the shore,
And the great gull, that fisher free,
   Dives right down a yard or more.

With main and jib we bound along,
   Through showers of spray we rise and dip,
But as for making any song,
   That needs a sea apprenticeship.

And now we meet the ocean swell,
   The bow swings high up in the air,
My breath goes with it ! I know well
   The land is best for me, not there !

We islanders should love the sea,
   The fresh wind, coiled nets, ballast heap,

The full brown sail, but as for me,
Again within that harbour's lee,
  I let the sea-song go to sleep !

WILLIAM BELL SCOTT.

THE TIDE.

OBLIVIOUSLY we long sat there
Weaving lines to praise the sea,
Objecting still, we still compare,
And try to make the rhythm agree
Between the verses and the sea.
When we thus began, the wave
Drove the pebbles up the beach,
Then resilient to the main
Drew them with it back again :
Nor dreamt we where the tide might reach,
Till it was round us everywhere,
Deep enough to be our grave !
For this is still the destined way,
We are masters, yet the prey.

WILLIAM BELL SCOTT.

THE sun upon the white sea shone
Ripples like living arrows came right on ;
From rock to rock a mist harmoniously
United heaven and earth in silvery grey.

WILLIAM BELL SCOTT.

THE SEA.

THESE froward waves, we feign they try
To utter to us some mystery :
Such is the euphuistic game
We baffled poets follow :—
Pantheistic ! all the same,
Like the sounding cymbal hollow :—
We it is, and not the sea,
Long to speak out God's mystery :
Immense and world-old salt ocean,
With thy moon-adoring motion,
Thou hast nought to us to say,
We must speak and thou obey.

WILLIAM BELL SCOTT.

THE SEA-SHORE.

FLAKES of foam are flown from the ebb
　White runners along the beach,
Where yesterday's margin of crab's green claws
　And stubble and starfish bleach.

A filmy ship looms now and then
　From the point where the keen winds blow,
Ghostlike it hangs in the air, then fades
　Where the unknown keen winds go.

Wave after wave for ten thousand years
  Has furrowed the brown sand here,
Wave after wave under clouds and stars
  Has cried in the dead shore's ear.

WILLIAM BELL SCOTT.

REST here and look down on the tremulous deep
Where sea-weeds like dead Mænad's long locks sweep
  Over that dreadful floor of stagnant green
  Strewn with the bones of lovers that have been,
Nor ever yet can scarce be said to sleep.

WILLIAM BELL SCOTT.

THE winds quiring to the choral sea.

A. C. SWINBURNE.

TO-NIGHT shall echo back the sea's dull roar
With a vain wail from passion's tide strown shore,
Where the dishevelled sea-weed hates the sea.

D. G. ROSSETTI.

THEREFORE sound on, whether with crash and din
Of crested billows leaping to the beach,
Or the mild music of the ebbing wave.

E. H. BRODIE.

THE TURN OF THE TIDE.

THE tide is on the turn; the uncertain sea,
With heavy swell, is swaying listlessly;
The wandering waves, with soft and gentle plash,
Scarce dare to break the stillness, and the wash
Back from the shelving shore with dreamy rush
Of pebbles, dying to a dreamy hush,
Seems as the faintest echo of the roar
Of beating surf, that crashed upon the shore
But three brief hours ago.   With weird, wild cry
The gulls sweep circling through the troubled sky;
All else seems held in mystic silence still,
As 'neath the power of an enchanter's will.

But, lo ! from where the craggy forelands bound
The limits of the bay, a rushing sound
Is sudden borne upon the breeze, and wakes
The sea from slumber, and like magic, breaks
The spell that holds the waves.   Each billow's crest
Is filled with life, and strives above the rest
To rear his frothy top; then rushes on,
In foaming haste, until the shore is won;
To waste its fury 'gainst some sea-worn rock
That countless ages has withstood the shock
Of rushing waves, and hurled them back again
To meet the inflowing current of the main.

R. F. S.

THE SEA-SPELL.

How oft the strange magnetic glamour of the Sea,
  The strange magnetic magic of her thrilling Voice,
Have won me, when 'mid lonely places, wild and free
  As any wandering wind, I have heard along the shore
  The wondrous, ever-varying Sea-Song loud rejoice.
  I have seen a stormy petrel, arising, poise
  Above the green-sloped wave, then pass for evermore
From keenest sight, and I have thought that I might be
Thus also deathward lured by glamour of the Sea.

WILLIAM SHARP.

ATLANTIC COMBERS.

THE pure green waves !—with crests of dazzling foam
      ashine,
  Onward they roll : innumerably grand, they beat
A wild and jubilant triumph-music all divine !
    The seafowl, their white kindred of the spray-swept
      air,
    Scream joyous echoes as with wave-dipped pinions
      fleet
    They whirl before the blast, or vanish 'mid blown sleet :
    In loud-resounding, strenuous, conquering play they
      fare,
Like clouds, high over dead forgotten lands i' the brine—
Great combing deep-sea waves with sunlit foam ashine.

WILLIAM SHARP.

THE SEA IN BONDAGE.

HARK to the long resilient surge o' the ebbing tide :
   With shingly rush and roar it foams adown the strand :
The great Sea heaves her restless bosom far and wide—
   Heedless she seems of winds and all the forceful laws
   That bar her empire over the usurping Land :
   Enough, she dreams, is her imperial command
   To make the very torrents, waveward falling, pause :
She scorns the Bridegroom-Land, yet is a subject Bride,
For She must come and go with each recurrent tide.

WILLIAM SHARP.

THE SWIMMER AT SUNRISE.

WHILE still the dusk impends above the glimmering waste,
   A tremor comes—wave after wave turns silvery bright--
A sudden yellow gleam athwart the east is traced—
   The waning stars fade forth, swift-perishing pyres—
   The moon lies pearly-wan upon the front of Night :
   Then all at once upswells a flood of golden light
   And a myriad waves flash forth a myriad fires :
Now is the hour the amplest glory of life to taste,
Out-swimming towards the sun upon the billowy waste !

WILLIAM SHARP.

THE TIDES OF VENICE.

WITH a soft, slow, gentle motion
    Swings the slow tide from the sea,
    Swings the slow tide hushfully
From the distant restless ocean,
    Through the sinuous canals
    Past the ancient wave-worn walls
That have seen the galleys sweep
With great captains of the deep,
    Fresh from where the Moslem calls
    The Muezzin from the steep
Temple-domes that face the sea.
    With a slow and gentle motion,
Like low breathing, ceaselessly
    The tide steals from the ocean,
    As a cloud that thro' the sky
    Ever draweth, draweth nigh
Though its white wings seem to beat
    No wind that blows at all,
But lie folded calm and sweet
By its soft immaculate side—
So moves the sleeping tide
    Past bridge and palace wall.
And hung in purple heaven,
    God's footstool, filled with light
And wheel'd by spirits seven,
    Seems the clear soul of night,
    So pure, so soft, so bright—

R

The very soul it seems
    Of Venice of the deep
    Lying hushed and still in sleep
'Neath the glory of her beams,
Dreaming, dreaming ancient dreams.
And like silver fires aglow
    The panting planets shine
And search the waters far below,
The waters that with stilly flow
      Come and go
    Beyond the salt sea-line.
A faint wind is playing
    With the small sea waves
    Above the myriad graves
O'er which move swaying, swaying
    The long green tangled reeds
    And grasses of the sea,
And softly stir the slimy weeds
That cling to where the salt sea laves
    The stairs of palaces that be
    No longer great or free.
At times, the shadows leaving,
    Black shapes leap forth and glide
    Like great fish on the tide—
    And singing side by side
The gondolieri, cleaving
    With lithe and rhythmic oar
The waters slowly heaving,
    Chant their old sea-born lore,
The old monotonous song
The tides have swept for long
    Round the Adriatic shore.
The very soul of mystery
    Seems brooding here alone :

Each bridge and pier and stone
Holds secrets of the sea ;
The slow tide hushfully
Moves with a scarce heard moan
And soft caressing motion,
For their past to it is known,
To it and the silent ocean.

* * * * *

Hush ! with what gentle swaying
The twilight waters go
As seaward still they flow ;
A new-born wind is playing
And singing weird strange runes
Out on the grey lagunes ;
And tolling to and fro,
With a music sad and slow,
A convent bell is ringing
O'er the cowled monks bent and singing—
Through the sinuous canals,
Past the ancient wave-worn walls
With a soft slow gentle motion
Swings the ebb tide to the sea,
Swings the slow tide hushfully
To the distant restless ocean.

WILLIAM SHARP.

ONE show'd an iron coast and angry waves,
You seem'd to hear them climb and fall
And roar rock-thwarted under bellowing caves,
Beneath the windy wall.

LORD TENNYSON.

MOONRISE AT SEA.

THE long slow swell of the still sea
Rises and falls, and sluggishly
The wind-bound ship rolls to and fro,
Soundless, save when the huge sails go
With heavy boom from left to right :
A few stars only trail their light
In quivering snaky gleams below
In the sea's depths, as though from caves
Within whose twilight glooms no waves
Move ever, serpents writhe and rise :
But westward far where sea and skies
Blend in one darkness, breaks a beam
Of wan faint light—and now a gleam,
Curv'd like a golden scimetar
And bright as though welded from a star,
Hangs for a moment, grows and grows
More round and large, a golden rose
Of one immaculate petal made :
And now the moon is risen, has laid
The magic of her musing smile
Upon the dim dark seas, till mile
On mile, league upon league, are bright
With a broad track of silver light,
And all the ships' sails seem to be
Of moon-beam gossamer woven free.

WILLIAM SHARP.

STORM IN THE TROPICS.

FROM "THE HUMAN INHERITANCE."

As the hot day swooned into afternoon
Hotter and hotter grew the air, and soon
All the north-western space of sky became
Heavy, metallic, where the heat did flame
In quivering bronze, and the sea grew changed
Tho' moveless still, as though dark rivers ranged
Purple and green and black throughout its deeps ;
At times, as a shudder comes o'er one who sleeps
And dreams of something evil, swiftly flew
Across its face a chill that changed the blue
To a sheet of beaten silver ; then again
It slept on as before, but as in pain.

And suddenly the ship's gun fired, and then
Three times the ensign dipped ; startled, the men
A moment stared, then down the shingly strand
Sped swiftly, and from the silvery sand
That edged the wave-line launched their boat and sprang
Each to his place, and soon there sharply rang
Through the electric air the cleaving oars
That swept them seaward from the island shores.

The sea seemed changed to oil, heavy and dark
And smooth, with frequently a blotch-like mark
Or stain, as though the lifeless waves had died
Of some disease and lain and putrefied.

And like a drop of oil, heavy and thick
A raindrop fell, making a sheeny flick
That glittered strangely ; then another came,
Another, and another, till a flame
Of pale wan light flickered above the waves
That slept, or lifeless lay, as over graves
New-made a ghastly glimmer drifts and gleams,
Or as that vagrant fire that faintly streams
O'er lonely marsh-lands thro' each swarthy night.
There was a strange, weird, calm, unearthly light
Shifting about the sky, as o'er the face
Of one who had been fair a smile might chase
The horror of some madness half away.
The rain-drops ceased : from the boat's oars the spray
Fell heavily : and then once more it rained
Slow drops awhile the boat's crew gained
The ship, where all with waiting anxious eyes
Watched the metallic gloom of brazen skies.

And suddenly there crashed a dreadful peal
Right overhead, the whole world seemed to reel
And stagger with the blow: the heaven's womb
Opened and brought forth flame : an awful gloom
Stretched like a pall and shrouded up the sun :
Then once again the thunder seem'd to stun
The shaking firmament, and livid jags
Of lightning tore the cloud-pall into rags—
Again and yet again as tho' 'twere hurled
Straight down for the destruction of the world,
And yet again like hell's fire uncontrolled :
And ceaselessly the deafening thunder rolled

Above and all around, as though the ship
Was in the hollow of God's hand, whose grip
Would close ere long and into powder grind.
At last burst forth the fury of the wind
Imprison'd long, which like a wild beast sprang
Upon the panting sea and howling swang
Its great frame to and fro, and yelled and tore
Its heaving breast, tossing thick foam like gore
In savage glee about ; and like a spray
Of blossom whirled before a gale, away
The ship was swept o'er boiling seas that fled
Before the wild wind howling as it sped
Far from its thunderous caverns overhead.

WILLIAM SHARP.

HE far away beheld the sea
Guarding the sweet land patiently.

WILLIAM MORRIS.

GLAMOUR of sea waves petulant and tender.

J. A. SYMONDS.

ONE night of storm
When the sky murmur'd, and the foamy sea
Flash'd in the fireflaugh round the shadowy cliffs.

ROBERT BUCHANAN.

WITH a dazzling glare
The sleeping ocean heaved his bosom bare :
. . . . .   Far in cool depths beneath
'Mid swaying loveliness of ocean-weed,
Bright fish swam to and fro, and with dire speed
The pale shark gleamed and vanished.

WILLIAM SHARP.

OH ! the immense, illimitable delight
  It is, to stand by some tempestuous bay,
What time the great sea waxes warm and white
  And beats and blinds the following wind with spray.

PHILIP BOURKE MARSTON.

BARE, as a wild wave in the wide North-Sea,
Green-glimmering toward the summit, bears, with all
Its stormy crests that smoke against the skies,
Down on a bark.

LORD TENNYSON.

AH, mighty boisterous blown breath, your siren song for
  me !
I quaff exhilarating draughts of wine from forth the sea,
Soft seething masses of fair froth luring deliciously !

HON. RODEN NOEL.

FROM " A HYMN TO THE SEA. '

I SAUNTER by the shore and lose myself
In the blue waters, stretching on, and on,
Beyond the low-lying headland, dark with woods,
And on to the green waste of sea, content
To be alone—but I am not alone,
For solitude like this is populous,
And its abundant life of sky and sun,
High-floating clouds, low mists, and wheeling birds,
And waves that ripple shoreward all day long,
Whether the tide is setting in or out,
Forever rippling shoreward, dark and bright,
As lights and shadows and the shifting winds
Pursue each other in their endless play,
Is more than the companionship of man.

*　　*　　*　　*　　*　　*

But thou, O Sea, whose majesty and might
Are mild and beautiful in this still bay,
But terrible in the mid-ocean deeps,
I never see thee but my soul goes out
To thee, and is sustained and comforted ;
For she discovers in herself, or thee,
A stern necessity for stronger life,
And strength to live it : she surrenders all
She had, and was, and is possessed of more,
With more to come—endurance, patience, peace.

I love thee, Ocean, and delight in thee,
Thy colour, motion, vastness,—all the eye
Takes in from shore, and on the tossing waves ;
Nothing escapes me, not the least of weeds
That shrivels and blackens on the barren sand.
I have been walking on the yellow sands,
Watching the long, white, ragged fringe of foam
The waves had washed up on the curves of beach,
The endless fluctuation of the waves,
The circuit of the seagulls, low, aloft,
Dipping their wings an instant in the brine,
And urging their swift flight to distant woods.
And round and over all the perfect sky,
Clear, cloudless, luminous in the summer noon.

* * * * * *

Thou wert before the Continents, before
The hollow heavens, which like another sea
Encircles them, and thee ; but whence thou wert,
And when thou wast created, is not known.
Antiquity was young when thou wast old.
There is no limit to thy strength, no end
To thy magnificence. Thou goest forth
On thy long journeys to remotest lands,
And comest back unwearied. Tropic isles,
Thick-set with pillared palms, delay thee not,
Nor arctic icebergs hasten thy return.
Summer and winter are alike to thee,
The settled sullen sorrow of the sky
Empty of light ; the laughter of the sun ;
The comfortable murmur of the wind
From peaceful countries, and the mad uproar

That storms let loose upon thee in the night
Which they create and quicken with sharp white fire,
And crash of thunders ! Thou art terrible
In thy tempestuous moods, when the loud winds
Precipitate their strength against the waves ;
They rave, and grapple and wrestle, until at last,
Baffled by their own violence, they fall back,
And thou art calm again, no vestige left
Of the commotion, save the long, slow roll
In summer days on beaches far away.

The heavens look down and see themselves in thee,
And splendours seen not elsewhere, that surround
The rising and the setting of the sun
Along thy vast and solitary realms.
The blue dominion of the air is thine,
And thine the pomps and pageants of the day,
The light, the glory, the magnificence,
The congregated masses of the clouds,
Islands, and mountains, and long promontories,
Floating at inaccessible heights whereto
Thy fathomless deeps are shallow—all are thine.
And thine the silent, happy, awful night,
When over thee and thy charmed waves the moon
Rides high, and when the last of stars is gone,
And darkness covers all things with its pall—
Darkness that was before the worlds were made,
And will be after they are dead.

R. H. STODDARD.

BY THE NORTH SEA.

I.

A LAND that is lonelier than ruin ;
 A sea that is stranger than death :
Far fields that a rose never blew in,
 Wan waste where the winds lack breath ;
Waste endless and boundless and flowerless
 But of marsh-blossoms fruitless as free :
Where earth lies exhausted, as powerless
  To strive with the sea.

Far flickers the flight of the swallows,
 Far flutters the weft of the grass
Spun dense over desolate hollows
 More pale than the clouds as they pass :
Thick woven as the weft of a witch is
 Round the heart of a thrall that hath sinned,
Whose youth and the wrecks of its riches
  Are waifs on the wind.

The pastures are herdless and sheepless,
 No pasture or shelter for herds :
The wind is relentless and sleepless,
 And restless and songless the birds ;
Their cries from afar fall breathless,
 Their wings are as lightnings that flee ;
For the land has two lords that are deathless :
  Death's self and the sea.

These twain, as a king with his fellow,
  Hold converse of desolate speech :
And her waters are haggard and yellow
  And crass with the scurf of the beach :
And his garments are grey as the hoary
  Wan sky where the day lies dim ;
And his power is to her, and his glory,
      As hers unto him.

In the pride of his power she rejoices,
  In her glory he glows and is glad :
In her darkness the sound of his voice is,
  With his breath she dilates and is mad :
'If thou slay me, O death, and outlive me,
  Yet thy love hath fulfilled me of thee.'
'Shall I give thee not back if thou give me,
      O sister, O sea ?'

And year upon year dawns living,
  And age upon age drops dead :
And his hand is not weary of giving,
  And the thirst of her heart is not fed :
And the hunger that moans in her passion,
  And the rage in her hunger that roars
As a wolf that the winter lays lash on,
      Still calls and implores.

Her walls have no granite for girder,
  No fortalice fronting her stands :
But reefs the bloodguiltiest of murder
  Are less than the banks of her sands :

These number their slain by the thousand ;
  For the ship hath no surety to be,
When the bank is abreast of her bows and
    Aflush with the sea.

No surety to stand, and no shelter
  To dawn out of darkness but one,
Out of waters that hurtle and welter
  No succour to dawn with the sun
But a rest from the wind as it passes,
  Where, hardly redeemed from the waves,
Lie thick as the blades of the grasses
    The dead in their graves.

A multitude noteless of numbers,
  As wild weeds cast on a heap :
And sounder than sleep are their slumbers,
  And softer than song is their sleep ;
And sweeter than all things and stranger
  The sense, if perchance it may be,
That the wind is divested of danger
    And scatheless the sea.

That the roar of the banks they breasted
  Is hurtless as bellowing of herds,
And the strength of his wings that invested
  The wind, as the strength of a bird's ;
As the seamew's might or the swallow's
  That cry to him back if he cries,

As over the graves and their hollows
Days darken and rise.

As the souls of the dead men disburdened
And clean of the sins they have sinned,
With a lovelier than man's life guerdoned
And delight as a wave's in the wind,
And delight as the wind's in the billow,
Birds pass, and deride with their glee
The flesh that has dust for its pillow
As wrecks have the sea.

When the ways of the sun wax dimmer,
Wings flash through the dusk like beams;
And the clouds in the lit sky glimmer,
The bird in the graveyard gleams;
As the cloud at its wing's edge whitens
When the clarions of sunrise are heard,
The graves that the bird's note brightens
Grow bright for the bird.

As the waves of the numberless waters
That the wind cannot number who guides
Are the sons of the shore and the daughters
Here lulled by the chime of the tides:
And here in the press of them standing
We know not if these or if we
Live trueliest, or anchored to landing
Or drifted to sea.

In the valley he named of decision
　　No denser were multitudes met
When the soul of the seer in her vision
　　Saw nations for doom of them set ;
Saw darkness in dawn, and the splendour
　　Of judgment, the sword and the rod,
But the doom here of death is more tender
　　And gentler the god.

And gentler the wind from the dreary
　　Sea-banks by the waves overlapped,
Being weary, speaks peace to the weary
　　From slopes that the tide-stream hath sapped;
And sweeter than all that we call so
　　The seal of their slumber shall be
Till the graves that embosom them also
　　Be sapped of the sea.

A. C. SWINBURNE.

AND on the sounding soft funereal shore
They, watching till the day should wholly die,
Saw the far sea sweep to the far grey sky,
Saw the long sands sweep to the long grey sea.
And night made one sweet mist of moor and lea,
And only far off shore the foam gave light.

A. C. SWINBURNE.

BY THE NORTH SEA.

III.

MILES, and miles, and miles of desolation !
   Leagues on leagues on leagues without a cha nge !
Sign or token of some eldest nation
   Here would make the strange land not so strange.
Time-forgotten, yea since time's creation,
   Seem these borders where the sea-birds range.

Slowly, gladly, full of peace and wonder
   Grows his heart who journeys here alone.
Earth and all its thoughts of earth sink under
   Deep as deep in water sinks a stone.
Hardly knows it if the rollers thunder,
   Hardly whence the lonely wind is blown.

Tall the plumage of the rush-flower tosses,
   Sharp and soft in many a curve and line
Gleam and glow the sea-coloured marsh-mosses,
   Salt and splendid from the circling brine.
Streak on streak of glimmering seashine crosses
   All the land sea-saturate as with wine.

Far, and far between, in divers orders
   Clear grey steeples cleave the low grey sky ;
Fast and firm as time-unshaken warders,
   Hearts made sure by faith, by hope made high.

These alone in all the wild sea-borders
  Fear no blast of days and nights that die.

All the land is like as one man's face is,
  Pale and troubled still with change of cares.
Doubt and death pervade her clouded spaces:
  Strength and length of life and peace are theirs;
Theirs alone amid these weary places,
  Seeing not how the wild world frets and fares.

Firm and fast where all is cloud that changes
  Cloud-clogged sunlight, cloud by sunlight thinned,
Stern and sweet, above the sand-hill ranges
  Watch the towers and tombs of men that sinned
Once, now calm as earth whose only change is
  Wind, and light, and wind, and cloud, and wind.

Out and in and out the sharp straits wander,
  In and out and in the wild way strives,
Starred and paved and lined with flowers that squander
  Gold as golden as the gold of hives
Salt and moist and multiform: but yonder,
  See, what sign of life or death survives?

Seen then only when the songs of olden
  Harps were young whose echoes yet endure,
Hymned of Homer when his years were golden,
  Known of only when the world was pure,
Here is Hades, manifest, beholden,
  Surely, surely here, if aught be sure!

Where the border-line was crossed, that, sundering
  Death from life, keeps weariness from rest,
None can tell, who fare here forward wondering ;
  None may doubt but here might end his quest.
Here life's lightning joys and woes once thundering
  Sea-like round him cease like storm suppressed.

Here the wise wave-wandering steadfast-hearted
  Guest of many a lord of many a land
Saw the shape or shade of years departed,
  Saw the semblance risen and hard at hand,
Saw the mother long from love's reach parted,
  Anticleia, like a statue stand.

Statue ? nay, nor tissued image woven
  Fair on hangings in his father's hall,
Nay, too fast her faith of heart was proven,
  Far too firm her loveliest love of all;
Love wherethrough the loving heart was cloven,
  Love that hears not when the loud Fates call.

Love that lives and stands up re-created
  Then when life has ebbed and anguish fled ;
Love more strong than death or all things fated,
  Child's and mother's, lit by love and led ;
Love that found what life so long awaited
  Here, when life came down among the dead.

Here, where never came alive another,
  Came her son across the sundering tide

Crossed before by many a warrior brother
  Once that warred on Ilion at his side ;
Here spread forth vain hands to clasp the mother
  Dead, that sorrowing for his love's sake died.

Parted, though by narrowest of divisions,
  Clasp he might not, only might implore,
Sundered yet by bitterest of derisions,
  Son, and mother from the son she bore—
Here ? But all dispeopled here of visions
  Lies, forlorn of shadows even, the shore.

All too sweet such men's Hellenic speech is,
  All too fain they lived of light to see,
Once to see the darkness of these beaches,
  Once to sing this Hades found of me
Ghostless, all its gulfs and creeks and reaches,
  Sky, and shore, and cloud, and waste, and sea !

A. C. SWINBURNE.

VAPOROUS blast ! voice of vast long sibilant sea-thunder !

HON. RODEN NOEL.

Now to the rugged cliff
The delicate foam with humid kisses clung,
And now retreated coy.

R. GARNETT.

SUNRISE AT SEA.

FROM "TRISTRAM OF LYONESSE."

THE quick sea shone
And shivered like spread wings of angels blown
By the sun's breath before him; and a low
Sweet gale shook all the foam-flowers of thin snow
As into rainfall of sea-roses shed
Leaf by wild leaf on that green garden-bed
Which tempests till and sea-winds turn and plough :
For rosy and fiery round the running prow
Fluttered the flakes and feathers of the spray,
And bloomed like blossoms cast by God away
To waste on the ardent water ; swift the moon
Withered to westward as a face in swoon
Death-stricken by glad tidings : and the height
Throbbed and the centre quivered with delight
And the depth quailed with passion as of love,
Till like the heart of some new-mated dove
Air, light, and wave seemed full of burning rest,
With motion as of one God's beating breast.

A. C. SWINBURNE.

SEA AND SUNRISE.

FROM " TRISTRAM OF LYONESSE."

So awhile

He watched the dim sea with a deepening smile,
And felt the sound and savour and swift flight
Of waves that fled beneath the fading night
And died before the darkness, like a song
With harps between and trumpets blown along
Through the loud air of some triumphant day,
Sink through his spirit and purge all sense away
Save of the glorious gladness of his hour
And all the world about to break in flower
Before the sovereign laughter of the sun ;
And he, ere night's wide work lay all undone,
As earth from her bright body casts off night,
Cast off his raiment for a rapturous fight
And stood between the sea's edge and the sea
Naked, and godlike of his mould as he
Whose swift foot's sound shook all the towers of Troy ;
So clothed with might, so girt upon with joy,
As, ere the knife had shorn to feed the fire
His glorious hair before the unkindled pyre
Whereon the half of his great heart was laid,
Stood, in the light of his live limbs arrayed,
Child of heroic earth and heavenly sea,
The flower of all men : scarce less bright than he,
If any of all men latter-born might stand,

Stood Tristram, silent, on the glimmering strand.
Not long : but with a cry of love that rang
As from a trumpet golden-mouthed, he sprang,
As toward a mother's where his head might rest
Her child rejoicing, toward the strong sea's breast
That none may gird nor measure : and his heart
Sent forth a shout that bade his lips not part,
But triumphed in him silent : no man's voice,
No song, no sound of clarions that rejoice,
Can set that glory forth which fills with fire
The body and soul that have their whole desire
Silent, and freer than birds or dreams are free
Take all their will of all the encountering sea.
And toward the foam he bent and forward smote,
Laughing, and launched his body like a boat
Full to the sea-breach, and against the tide
Struck strongly forth with amorous arms made wide
To take the bright breast of the wave to his
And on his lips the sharp sweet minute's kiss
Given of the wave's lip for a breath's space curled
And pure as at the daydawn of the world.
And round him all the bright rough shuddering sea
Kindled, as though the world were even as he,
Heart-stung with exultation of desire :
And all the life that moved him seemed to aspire,
As all the sea's life toward the sun : and still
Delight within him waxed with quickening will
More smooth and strong and perfect as a flame
That springs and spreads, till each glad limb became
A note of rapture in the tune of life,
Live music mild and keen as sleep and strife :
Till the sweet change that bids the sense grow sure
Of deeper depth and purity more pure
Wrapped him and lapped him round with clearer cold,

And all the rippling green grew royal gold
Between him and the far sun's rising rim.
And like the sun his heart rejoiced in him,
And brightened with a broadening flame of mirth :
And hardly seemed its life a part of earth,
But the life kindled of a fiery birth
And passion of a new-begotten son
Between the live sea and the living sun.
And mightier grew the joy to meet full-faced
Each wave, and mount with upward plunge, and taste
The rapture of its rolling strength, and cross
Its flickering crown of snows that flash and toss
Like plumes in battle's blithest charge, and thence
To match the next with yet more strenuous sense ;
Till on his eyes the light beat hard and bade
His face turn west and shoreward through the glad
Swift revel of the waters golden-clad,
And back with light reluctant heart he bore
Across the broad-backed rollers in to shore ;
Strong-spirited for the chance and cheer of fight,
And donned his arms again, and felt the might
In all his limbs rejoice for strength, and praised
God for such life as that whereon he gazed.

A. C. SWINBURNE.

THE salt shore, furrowed by the foam, smells sweet.

P. B. MARSTON.

THE COMING OF STORM.

FROM "TRISTRAM OF LYONESSE."

AND while they sat at speech as at a feast,
Came a light wind fast hardening forth of the east
And blackening till its might had marred the skies ;
And the sea thrilled as with heart-sundering sighs
One after one drawn, with each breath it drew,
And the green hardened into iron blue,
And the soft light went out of all its face.
Then Tristram girt him for an oarsman's place
And took his oar and smote, and toiled with might
In the east wind's full face and the strong sea's spite
Labouring ; and all the rowers rowed hard, but he
More mightily than any wearier three.
And Iseult watched him rowing with sinless eyes
That loved him but in holy girlish wise
For noble joy in his fair manliness
And trust and tender wonder ; none the less
She thought if God had given her grace to be
Man, and make war on danger of earth and sea,
Even such a man she would be ; for his stroke
Was mightiest as the mightier water broke,
And in sheer measure like strong music drave
Clean through the wet weight of the wallowing wave,
And as a tune before a great king played
For triumph was the tune their strong strokes made,
And sped the ship through with smooth strife of oars

Over the mid sea's grey foam-paven floors,
For all the loud breach of the waves at will.
So for an hour they fought the storm out still,
And the shorn foam spun from the blades, and high
The keel sprang from the wave-ridge, and the sky
Glared at them for a breath's space through the rain.

A. C. SWINBURNE.

HARD by the sea
Made a noise like the aspens.

WILLIAM MORRIS.

THE sky leans dumb on the sea,
    Aweary with all its wings ;
    And oh ! the song the sea sings
Is dark everlastingly.

D. G. ROSSETTI.

I HEAR the wan waves sobbing on the shore.

PHILIP B. MARSTON.

THE LAST SLEEP OF TRISTRAM AND ISEULT.

AND round the sleep that fell around them then
Earth lies not wrapped, nor records wrought of men
Rise up for timeless token : but their sleep
Hath round it like a raiment all the deep ;
No change or gleam or gloom of sun and rain,
But all time long the might of all the main
Spread round them as round earth soft heaven is spread,
And peace more strong than death round all the dead.
For death is of an hour, and after death
Peace : nor for aught that fear or fancy saith,
Nor even for very love's own sake, shall strife
Perplex again that perfect peace with life.
And if, as men that mourn may deem or dream,
Rest haply here than there might sweeter seem,
And sleep, that lays one hand on all, more good
By some sweet grave's grace given of wold or wood
Or clear high glen or sunbright wind-worn down
Than where life thunders through the trampling town
With daylong feet and nightlong overhead,
What grave may cast such grace round any dead,
What so sublime sweet sepulchre may be
For all that life leaves mortal, as the sea ?
And these, rapt forth perforce from earthly ground,
These twain the deep sea guards, and girdles round
Their sleep more deep than any sea's gulf lies,
Though changeless with the change in shifting skies,
Nor mutable with seasons : for the grave

That held them once, being weaker than a wave,
The waves long since have buried : though their tomb
Was royal that by ruth's relenting doom
Men gave them in Tintagel : for the word
Took wing which thrilled all piteous hearts that heard
The word wherethrough their lifelong lot stood shown,
And when the long sealed springs of fate were known,
The blind bright innocence of lips that quaffed
Love, and the marvel of the mastering draught,
And all the fraughtage of the fateful bark,
Loud like a child upon them wept King Mark,
Seeing round the sword's hilt which long since had fought
For Cornwall's love a scroll of writing wrought,
A scripture writ of Tristram's hand, wherein
Lay bare the sinless source of all their sin,
No choice of will, but chance and sorcerous art,
With prayer of him for pardon : and his heart
Was molten in him, wailing as he kissed
Each with the kiss of kinship—"Had I wist,
Ye had never sinned nor died thus, nor had I
Borne in this doom that bade you sin and die
So sore a part of sorrow."　And the king
Built for their tomb a chapel bright like spring
With flower-soft wealth of branching tracery made
Fair as the frondage each fleet year sees fade,
That should not fall till many a year were done.
There slept they wedded under moon and sun
And change of stars : and through the casements came
Midnight and noon girt round with shadow and flame
To illume their grave or veil it : till at last
On these things too was doom as darkness cast :
For the strong sea hath swallowed wall and tower,
And where their limbs were laid in woful hour
For many a fathom gleams and moves and moans

The tide that sweeps above their coffined bones
In the wrecked chancel by the shivered shrine :
Nor where they sleep shall moon or sunlight shine
Nor man look down for ever : none shall say,
Here once, or here, Tristram and Iseult lay :
But peace they have that none may gain who live,
And rest about them that no love can give,
And over them, while death and life shall be,
The light and sound and darkness of the sea.

A. C. SWINBURNE.

THE sea
Sighed further off eternally
As human sorrow sighs in sleep.

D. G. ROSSETTI.

BUT evermore
Most weary seem'd the sea, weary the oar,
Weary the wandering fields of barren foam.

LORD TENNYSON.

THE SEA CALLS.

v.

THOU art not clamorous.   Nay, thy silvery tongue
  And rhetoric that holds me night and noon
  Attentive to one tender monotone,
  Are clear as fairy chimes by lilies rung.
They speak of twilight and grave ditties sung
  By seamen brown beneath a low broad moon,
  And breezes with the sea-scent in them blown
  At sundown, when the few faint stars are hung
Dim overhead in fields of hyacinth blue ;
  When, lifted between sea and sky, those isles
  North-gazing change from rose and blossoming rue
To privet paleness ; and dark harbour piles
  Bar the wide fire-irradiate west ; wherethrough
  Declining day, like a dead hero, smiles.

J. A. SYMONDS.

STELLA MARIS

IV.

FAIR is the sea ; and fair the sea-borne billow,
  Blue from the depth and curled with crested argent :
  Fair is the sea ; and fair the smooth sea-margent,
  The brown dunes waved with tamarisk and willow :
Fair is the sea ; and fair the seaman's daughter,
  Fairer than all fair things in earth and ocean :
  Fair is the sea ; and fair the wayward motion,
  The wavering glint of light on dancing water :
Fair is the sea ; and fair the heavens above it,
  And fair at ebb the grass-green wildernesses ;
  Fair is the sea ; and fair the stars that love it,
Rising from waves new-washed with orient tresses :
  Fair is the sea ; of all fair sea-things fairest,
  Stella, thou sea-born star art best and rarest.

J. A. SYMONDS.

A DREAM OF BURIAL IN MID-OCEAN.

Down through the deep deep grey-green seas, in sleep,
 Plunged my drowsed soul; and ever on and on,
 Hurrying at first, then where the faint light shone
Through fathoms twelve, with slackening fall did creep,
Nor touched the bottom of that bottomless steep,
 But with a slow sustained suspension,
 Buoyed 'mid the watery wildernesses wan,
Like a thin cloud in air, voyaged the deep.

Then all those dreadful faces of the sea,
 Horned things abhorred and shapes intolerable,
 Fixing glazed lidless eyes swam up to me,
And pushed me with their snouts, and coiled and fell
 In spiral volumes writhing horribly—
 Jagged fins grotesque, fanged ghastly jaws of hell.

J. A. Symonds.

VENETIAN SUNRISE.

How often have I now outwatched the night
   Alone in this grey chamber toward the sea
   Turning its deep-arcaded balcony !
Round yonder sharp acanthus-leaves the light
Comes stealing, red at first, then golden bright ;
   Till when the day-god in his strength and glee
   Springs from the orient flood victoriously,
Each cusp is tipped and tongued with quivering white.
The islands that were blots of purple bloom,
   Now tremble in soft liquid luminous haze,
   Uplifted from the sea-floor to the skies ;
And dim discerned erewhile through roseate gloom,
   A score of sails now stud the waterways,
   Ruffling like swans afloat from paradise.

J. A. Symonds.

WIND AND SEA.

THE sea is a jovial comrade,
   He laughs wherever he goes ;
His merriment shines in the dimpling lines
   That wrinkle his hale repose ;
He lays himself down at the feet of the Sun,
   And shakes all over with glee
And the broad-backed billows fall faint on the shore,
   In the mirth of the mighty sea !

But the wind is sad and restless,
   And cursed with an inward pain ;
You may hark at will, by valley or hill,
   But you hear him still complain.
He wails on the barren mountains
   And shrieks on the wintry sea ;
He sobs in the cedar and moans in the pine,
   And shudders all over the aspen tree.

Welcome are both their voices,
   And I know not which is best,—
The laughter that slips from Ocean's lips,
   Or the comfortless wind's unrest.
There's a pang in all rejoicing
   A joy in the heart of pain,
And the wind that saddens, the sea that gladdens,
   Are singing the self-same strain.

BAYARD TAYLOR.

THE SEA SHELL: FROM "MAUD."

See what a lovely shell,
Small and pure as a pearl,
Lying close to my foot,
Frail, but a work divine,
Made so fairily well
With delicate spire and whorl,
How exquisitely minute
A miracle of design !

*   *   *   *

The tiny cell is forlorn,
Void of the little living will
That made it stir on the shore.
Did he stand at the diamond door
Of his house in a rainbow frill ?
Did he push, when he was uncurl'd,
A golden foot or a fairy horn
Thro' his dim water-world ?

Slight, to be crush'd with a tap
Of my finger-nail on the sand,
Small, but a work divine,
Frail, but of force to withstand,
Year upon year, the shock
Of cataract seas, that snap
The three-decker's oaken spine
Athwart the ledges of rock,
Here on the Breton strand !

Lord Tennyson.

FROM "THE PALACE OF ART."

A STILL salt pool, lock'd in with bars of sand ;
  Left on the shore ; that hears all night
The plunging seas draw backward from the land
  Their moon-led waters white.

LORD TENNYSON.

FROM "SEA-DREAMS."

A FULL-TIDE

Rose with ground swell, which, on the foremost rocks
Touching, upjetted in spirts of wild sea-smoke
And scaled in sheets of wasteful foam and fell
In vast sea-cataracts—ever and anon
Dead claps of thunder from within the cliffs
Heard thro' the living roar.

LORD TENNYSON.

FROM "ELEÄNORE.'

As waves that up a quiet cove
  Rolling slide, and lying still
  Shadow forth the banks at will :
Or sometimes they swell and move,
  Pressing up against the land,
  With motions of the outer sea.

LORD TENNYSON.

FROM "A DREAM OF FAIR WOMEN."

WHEN to land
Bluster the winds and tides the self-same way,
Crisp foam-flakes scud along the level sand,
Torn from the fringe of spray.

LORD TENNYSON.

AND did you never lie upon the shore
And watch the curl'd white of the coming wave
Glass'd in the slippery sand before it breaks?

LORD TENNYSON.

HALF lost in the liquid azure bloom of a crescent of sea,
The silent sapphire-spangled marriage ring of the land?

LORD TENNYSON.

THE deep
All down the sand,
Is breathing in his sleep,
Heard by the land.

LORD TENNYSON.

OFF SHORE.

Rock, little boat, beneath the quiet sky,
Only the stars behold us where we lie,—
Only the stars and yonder brightening moon.

On the wide sea to-night alone are we ;
The sweet, bright summer day dies silently,
Its glowing sunset will have faded soon.

Rock, softly, little boat, the while I mark
The far-off gliding sails, distinct and dark,
Across the west pass steadily and slow.

But on the eastern waters sad, they change
And vanish, dream-like, gray, and cold, and strange,
And no one knoweth whither they may go.

We care not, we, drifting with wind and tide,
While glad waves darken upon either side,
Save where the moon sends silver sparkles down.

And yonder slender stream of changing light,
Now white, now crimson, tremulously bright,
Where dark the light-house stands with fiery crown.

Thick falls the dew, soundless on sea and shore :
It shines on little boat and idle oar,
Wherever moonbeams touch with tranquil glow.

The waves are full of whispers wild and sweet ;
They call to me,—incessantly they beat
Along the boat from stern to curved prow.

Comes the careering wind, blows back my hair
All damp with dew to kiss me unaware,
Murmuring " Thee I love," and passes on.

Sweet sounds on rocky shores the distant note ;
O could we float forever, little boat,
Under the blissful sky drifting alone.

CELIA THAXTER.

THIS way and that the leaden seas were hurled,
Moved by no wind, but by some unseen power.

WILLIAM MORRIS.

FAR off, the silent sea gloomed cold and gray,
Sky-sundered by one long low line of white.

ALFRED AUSTIN.

A BATHING SNATCH.

O SUN, lay down thy golden bridge
   Across the waters clear !
O foam, flash round each rock and ridge
   That soon shall disappear !
O tide, swell up a full spring-tide
   Upon the shingly shore !
For, oh, I love thy surge-sweep wide
   And long-resounding roar !

JAMES THOMSON.

BY THE SEA.

I

THE burning golden Rose of the Day
 Droops down to the Western sea ;
And the amber and purple flush of the sky
 And the crimson glow of the sea
Ebb, ebb away,—fade, fade and die ;
While the earth, all mantled in shadowy grey,
Washes her brow with a restful sigh
 In the cool sweet dews of the gloaming.

Then the shining silver Lily of the night
 Opens broad her leaves divine,
 Afloat on the azure hyaline
Of the heavenly sea ; and her purest light
Kisses the earth that dreaming lies
 In a still, enchanted sleeping ;
While the heavens with their countless starry eyes
 Still watch are keeping.

The Earth loves the golden Rose of the Day,
 From which she distils the fiery wine
Of immortal youth and magnificent might ;
But the Sea loves the silver Lily of the Night,
For her beams are as wands of a holier sway,
 Whose spell brings the trance divine :
The Rose for Life's feast and the festal array,
 The Lily for Death's shrine.

II.

THE earth lay breathless in a fever-swoon
   Beneath the burning noon,
Sun-stricken, dazed with light and sick with heat:
Then came the waters from the cool midsea
   Trooping up blithe and free,
And fanned her brow with airs so fresh and sweet,
And crept about her gently, and caressed
   Her broad unheaving breast
With the white cincture of a magic zone ;
Bathing and swathing her faint limbs, that were
   In the fierce sun-fire bare,
With lucid liquid folds of rich green purple strown.
Then as the sun went sinking to his rest
   Down the enamoured west,
The waves were leaving the calm earth to dreams ;
Bearing the smirch of the long day's turmoil,
   The sweat of her fierce toil,
The sultry breaths and languid, feverous streams ;
Bearing all far away, and as they went
   Whispering with blithe content,
To drown and cleanse them in the pure midsea :
The while the earth, all dewy sweet and clean,
   And drowsily serene
Beneath the star-dewed heavens might slumber safe
      and free.

JAMES THOMSON.

THE SEA KING.

From out his castle on the sand
He led his tawny-bearded band
In stormy bark from land to land.

The red dawn was his goodly sign :
He set his face to sleet and brine,
And quaffed the blast like ruddy wine.

And often felt the swirling gale
Beat, like some giant thresher's flail,
Upon his battered coat of mail.

Or sacked, at times, some windy town,
And from the pastures, parched and brown,
He drove the scurrying cattle down ;

And kissed the maids, and stole the bell
From off the church below the fell,
And drowned the priest within the well.

And he had seen, on frosty nights,
Strange, whirling forms and elfin sights,
In twilight land, by Northern Lights.

Or, sailing on by windless shoal,
Had heard, by night, the song of troll
Within some cavern-haunted knoll.

Off Iceland, too, the sudden rush
Of waters falling, in a hush
He heard the ice-fields grind and crush.

His prow the sheeny south seas clove ;
Warm, spicèd winds from lemon grove
And heated thicket round him drove.

The storm-blast was his deity ;
His lover was the fitful sea ;
The wailing winds his melody.

By rocky scaur and beachy head
He followed where his fancy led,
And down the rainy waters fled ;

And left the peopled towns behind,
And gave his days and nights to find
What lay beyond the western wind.

L. Frank Tooker.

THE ocean beats against the stern, dumb shore,
The stormy passion of its mighty heart.

L. C. Moulton.

HYMN TO OCEAN.

O CRADLE, whence the suns ascend, old Ocean divine ;
O grave, whereto the suns descend, old Ocean divine :

O spreading in the calm of night thy mirror, wherein
The Moon her countenance doth bend, old Ocean divine.

O thou that dost in midnights still thy chorus of waves
With dances of the planet blend, old Ocean divine :

The morning and the evening blooms are roses of thine,
Two roses that for thine are kenned, old Ocean divine.

O Aphrodite's panting breast, whose breathing doth make
The waves to fall and ascend, old Ocean divine.

O womb of Aphrodite, bear thy beautiful child,
Abroad thy glory to commend, old Ocean divine.

O sprinkle thou with pearly dew Earth's garland of
    spring,
For only thou hast pearls to spend, old Ocean divine.

All Naiads that from thee had sprung, commanded by thee
Back to thy Nereid-dances tend, old Ocean divine.

What ships of thought sail forth on thee ! Atlantis doth
    sleep
In silence at thine utmost end, old Ocean divine.

The goblets of the gods, from high Olympus that fall
Thou dost on coral boughs suspend, old Ocean divine.

A diver in the sea of love my song is, that fain
Thy glory would to all commend, old Ocean divine.

I, like the moon, beneath thy waves with yearning would
    plunge ;
Thence might I like the sun ascend, old Ocean divine.

RICHARD CHENEVIX TRENCH.

WHEN the great seas roar
Suck'd in thro' weedy rocks and undercaves
In hoarse and billowy breaths of solemn sound.

ROBERT BUCHANAN.

IN cadenced mirrors fall the sudden notes
Of waves o'erlapping waves, with echoes dim
From where in whispers on the gleaming sands
One longer dies in kisses, but beyond —
We hear the hollow booming in the caves
Where the great billows in an endless pæan
Surge in and out, and over all ring faint
The shrill harmonics of the plaining gulls.
There is the pain of something infinite
In the deep sea, and in its lonely waves,
A yearning unfulfilled, unsatisfied.

WILLIAM SHARP.

THE OCEAN.

The ocean at the bidding of the moon
For ever changes with his restless tide ;
Flung shoreward now, to be regathered soon
With kingly pauses of reluctant pride
And semblance of return : Anon—from home
He issues forth anew, high ridg'd and free—
The gentlest murmur of his seething foam
Like armies whispering where great echoes be !
O leave me here upon this beach to rove,
Mute listener to that sound so grand and lone—
A glorious sound, deep drawn and strongly thrown,
And reaching those on mountain heights above,
To British ears, (as who shall scorn to own ?)
A tutelar fond voice, a saviour-tone of Love !

CHARLES TENNYSON-TURNER.

THE BUOY-BELL.

How like the leper, with his own sad cry
  Enforcing its own solitude, it tolls !
  That lonely bell set in the rushing shoals,
To warn us from the place of jeopardy !
O friend of man ! sore-vexed by Ocean's power
  The changing tides wash o'er thee day by day ;
Thy trembling mouth is filled with bitter spray,
Yet still thou ringest on from hour to hour ;
High is thy mission, though thy lot is wild—
  To be in danger's realm a guardian sound ;
    In seaman's dreams a pleasant part to bear,
And earn their blessing as the year goes round ;
    And strike the key-note of each grateful prayer,
Breathed in their distant homes by wife or child.

CHARLES TENNYSON-TURNER.

THE QUIET TIDE NEAR ARDROSSAN.

On to the beach the quiet waters crept :
But, though I stood not far within the land,
No tidal murmur reach'd me from the strand.
The mirror'd clouds beneath old Arran slept.
I looked again across the watery waste :
The shores were full, the tide was near its height,
Though scarcely heard : the reefs were drowning fast,
And an imperial whisper told the might
Of outer floods, that press'd into the bay,
Though all besides was silent.   I delight
In the rough billows, and the foam-ball's flight :
I love the shore upon a stormy day ;
But yet more stately were the power and ease
That with a whisper deepen'd all the seas.

CHARLES TENNYSON-TURNER.

CHANGED VOICES.

LAST night the sea-wind was to me
A metaphor of liberty,
   And every wave along the beach
A starlit beauty seemed to be.

To-day the sea-wind is to me
A fettered soul that would be free,
   And dumbly striving after speech
The tides yearn landward painfully.

To-morrow how shall sound for me
The changing voice of wind and sea?
   What tidings shall be borne of each?
What rumour of what mystery?

WILLIAM WATSON.

U

THE SONG OF THE SEA.

Even as one voice the great sea sang.   From out
The green heart of the waters round about,
Welled as a bubbling fountain silverly
The overflowing song of the great sea ;
Until the Prince, by dint of listening long,
Divined the purport of that mystic song ;
(For so do all things breathe articulate breath
Into his ears who rightly hearkeneth :)
And, if indeed he heard that harmony
Aright, in this wise came the song of the sea.

" Behold all ye that stricken of love do lie,
Wherefore in manacles of a maiden's eye
Lead ye the life of bondmen and of slaves?
Lo, in the caverns and the depths of Me
A thousand mermaids dwell beneath the waves :
A thousand maidens meet for love have I,
Ev'n I the virgin-hearted cold chaste sea.

Behold all ye that weary of life do lie,
There is no rest at all beneath the sky
Save in the nethermost deepness of the deep.
Only the silence and the midst of Me
Can still the sleepless soul that fain would sleep ;
For such, a cool death and a sweet have I,
Ev'n I the crystal-hearted cool sweet sea.

Behold all ye that in my lap do lie,
To love is sweet and sweeter still to die,
And woe to him that laugheth me to scorn !
Lo in a little while the anger of Me
Shall make him mourn the day that he was born :
For in mine hour of wrath no ruth have I,
Ev'n I the tempest-hearted pitiless sea.'

WILLIAM WATSON.

AND as a full field charging was the sea,
And as the cry of slain men was the wind.

A. C. SWINBURNE.

EVEN as his who on some midnight hears
Upon a close, and yet night-hidden strand,
The roused sea calling to the silent land.

P. B. MARSTON

MURMURS and scents of the infinite Sea.

MATTHEW ARNOLD.

HEARS the low plash of wave o'erwhelming wave,
The loving lullaby of mother ocean.

SIR HENRY TAYLOR.

O SLEEP, thou hollow sea, thou soundless sea,
Dull-breaking on the shores of haunted lands,
Lo, I am thine : do what thou wilt with me.

But while, as yet unbounden of thy bands,
I hear the breeze from inland chide and chafe
Along the margin of thy muttering sands,

Somewhat I fain would crave, if thou vouchsafe
To hear mine asking, and to heed wilt deign.
Behold, I come to fling me as a waif

Upon thy waters, O thou murmuring main,
So on some wasteful island cast not me,
Where phantom winds to phantom skies complain,

And creeping terrors crawl from out the sea,
(For such thou hast)—but o'er thy waves not cold
Bear me to yonder land once more, where She

Sits throned amidst of magic wealth untold :
Golden her palace, golden all her hair,
Golden her city 'neath a heaven of gold !

So may I see in dreams her tresses fair
Down-falling, as a wave of sunlight rests
On some white cloud, about her shoulders bare,
Nigh to the snowdrifts twain which are her breasts.

WILLIAM WATSON.

A STARRY NIGHT AT SEA.

IF Heaven's bright halls are very far from sea
I dread a pang the angels could not suage :
The imprisoned sea-bird knows—and only he—
How azure-domed and bright may be a cage :
Between the bars he sees a prison still :—
The self-same wood or meadow or silver stream
That lends the captive lark a joyous thrill
Is landscape in the sea-bird's prison-dream :

So might I languish on yon starry floor,
Fainting for brine 'mid music of the spheres :
Billows like these that never knew a shore
Might mock mine eyes and tease my hungry ears :—
No scent of amaranths o'er yon glittering vault
Might quell this breath of Ocean sharp and salt.

THEODORE WATTS.

THE LIGHT-HOUSE GIRL.

I.

AMID the Channel's wiles and fell decoys
  Where " Casket Beacons " watch the Siren-sea,
  A girl was reared who knew nor flower nor tree
Nor breath of grass at dawn, yet had high joys :
The moving lawns whose verdure never cloys
  Were hers.   At last she sailed to Alderney,
  But there she pined. " *The bustling world,*" said she,
" *Is all too full of trouble and of noise.*"

The storm-child fainting for her home the storm
  Had winds for sponsors—one proud rock for nurse,
  Whose granite arms disperse and aye disperse
All billowy squadrons tide and wind can form :
No fever of Love she knew, nor Love's alarm :
  The Siren-sea was still her universe.

THE LIGHT-HOUSE GIRL.

II.

LOVE bringeth Fear with eyes of augury :—
   Her lover's boat was out : her ears were dinned
   With sea-sobs warning of the awaked wind
That shook the troubled sun's red canopy.
Even while she prayed the storm's high revelry
   Woke petrel, gull—all revellers wing'd and finn'd—
   And clutch'd a sail brown-patch'd and weather-
      thinned,
And then a swimmer fought a white wild sea.

" My songs are louder, child, than prayers of thine,"
   The Siren sang : " thy sea-boy waged no strife
   With Hatred's poison, gangrened Envy's knife :—
I strove with him, in deadly sport divine :—
   The old wrestle of the gods for light and life
Was his ; then peace within these arms of mine ! "

THEODORE WATTS.

A MORNING SWIM IN GUERNSEY.

I.

WE are in the " Coloured Caves " the sea-maid built ;
　Her walls are stained beyond that lonely fern,
　For she must fly at every tide's return,
And all her sea-tints round the walls are spilt.
Outside behold the bay, each headland gilt
　With morning's gold ; far off the foam-wreathes burn
　Like fiery snakes, while here the sweet waves yearn
Up sand more soft than Avon's sacred silt.

And smell the sea !　No breath from wood or field,
　No scent of may or rose or eglantine,
　Cuts off the old life where cities suffer and pine,
Shuts the dark house where Memory stands revealed,
Calms the vext spirit, balms a sorrow unhealed,
　Like scent of sea-weed rich of morn and brine.

A MORNING SWIM IN GUERNSEY.

II.

As if the Spring's fresh groves should change and shake
To dark green woods of cedar or terebinth,
Then break to bloom of amorous hyacinth,
So 'neath us change the waves, rising to take
Each kiss of colour from each cloud and flake
Round many a rocky hall and labyrinth,
Where sea-wrought column, arch, and granite plinth,
Show how the sea's fine rage dares make and break.

Young with the youth the immortal brine can lend,
Our glowing limbs, with sea and sun empearled,
Seem born anew, and in your eyes, dear friend,
Rare pictures shine—like faery flags unfurl'd—
Of child-land, where the roofs of rainbows bend
Over the golden wonders of the world.

THEODORE WATTS.

ODE TO MOTHER CAREY'S CHICKEN.

*(On seeing a Storm-Petrel in a cage on a cottage wall and
releasing it.)*

GAZE not at me, my poor unhappy bird;
 That sorrow is more than human in thine eye;
Too deep already is my spirit stirred
 To see thee here, child of the sea and sky,
Cooped in a cage with food thou canst not eat,
Thy "snow-flake" soiled, and soiled those conquering
  feet,
That walked the billows, while thy "*sweet-sweet-sweet*"
  Proclaimed the tempest nigh.

Bird whom I welcomed while the sailors cursed,
 Friend whom I blessed wherever keels may roam,
Prince of my childish dreams, whom mermaids nursed
 In purple of billows—silver of ocean-foam,
Abashed I stand before thy mighty grief—
Of sorrow's very king the king and chief :—
To ride the wind and hold the sea in fief,
  Then find a cage for home !

From out thy jail thou seest yon heath and woods,
   But canst thou hear the birds or smell the flowers ?
Ah, no ! those rain-drops twinkling on the buds
   Bring only visions of the salt sea-showers.
" The sea ! " the linnets pipe from hedge and heath ;
" The sea ! " the honey-suckles whisper and breathe ;
And tumbling waves, where those wild-roses wreathe,
   Murmur from dewy bowers.

These winds so soft to others,—how they burn !
   The mavis sings with gurgle and ripple and plash,
To thee yon swallow seems a wheeling tern.
   And when the rains recall the briny lash—
Old Ocean's kiss thou lovest,—when thy sight
Is mocked with Ocean's horses—manes of white,
The long and shadowy flanks, the shoulders bright—
   Bright as the lightning's flash,—

When all these scents of heather and brier and whin,
   All kindly breaths of land-shrub, flower, and vine,
Recall the sea-scents, till thy feathered skin
   Tingles in answer to a dream of brine,—
When thou, remembering there thy royal birth,
Dost see between the bars a world of dearth,
Is there a grief—a grief on all the earth—
   So heavy and dark as thine ?

But I can buy thy freedom—I (thank God !),
    Who loved thee more than albatross or gull—
Loved thee when on the waves thy footsteps trod—
    Dream'd of thee when, becalmed, we lay a-hull—
'Tis I thy friend who once, a child of six,
To find where Mother Carey fed her chicks,
Climbed up the stranded punt, and, with two sticks,
    Tried all in vain to scull,—

Thy friend who owned a Paradise of Storm—
    The little dreamer of the cliffs and coves,
Who knew thy mother, saw her shadowy form
    Behind the cloudy bastions where she moves,
And heard her call : " Come ! for the welkin thickens,
And tempests mutter and the lightning quickens ! "
Then, starting from his dream would find the chickens
    Were only blue rock-doves,—

Thy friend who owned another Paradise
    Of calmer air, a floating isle of fruit,
Where sang the nereids on a breeze of spice
    While Triton, from afar, would sound salute :
There wast thou winging, though the skies were calm,
For marvellous strains, as of the morning's shalm,
Were struck by ripples round that isle of palm
    Whose shores were " Carey's lute."

And now to see thee here, my king, my king,
    Far-glittering memories mirror'd in those eyes,
As if there shone within an iris-ring
    The orbèd world—ocean and hills and skies!—
Those black wings ruffled whose triumphant sweep
Conquered in sport!—yea, up the glimmering steep
Of highest billow, down the deepest deep,
        Sported with victories!

To see thee here!—a coil of wiltered weeds
    Beneath those feet that danced on diamond spray,
Rider of sportive Ocean's reinless steeds—
    Winner in Mother Carey's sabbath-fray
When, stung by magic of the witch's chant,
They rise, each foamy-crested combatant—
They rise and fall and leap and foam and gallop and pant
    Till albatross, sea-swallow, and cormorant
        Are scared like doves away!

And shalt thou ride no more where thou hast ridden,
    And feast no more in hyaline halls and caves,
Master of Mother Carey's secrets hidden,
    Master most equal of the wind and waves,
Who never, save in stress of angriest blast,
Asked ship for shelter,—never till at last
The foam-flakes hurled against the sloping mast
        Slashed thee like whirling flames?

Right home to fields no sea-mew ever kenned,
    Where scarce the great sea-wanderer fares with thee,
I come to take thee—nay, 'tis I, thy friend—
    Ah, tremble not—I come to set thee free ;
I come to tear this cage from off this wall,
And take thee hence to that fierce festival
Where billows march and winds are musical,
      Hymning the Victor-Sea !

    *   *   *   *

Yea, lift thine eyes, mine own can bear them now :
    Thou'rt free ! thou'rt free—ah, surely a bird can smile !
Dost know me, Petrel ?   Dost remember how
    I fed thee in the wake for many a mile,
Whilst thou wouldst pat the waves, then, rising, take
The morsel up and wheel about the wake ?
Thou'rt free, thou'rt free, but for thine own dear sake
      I keep thee caged awhile.

Away to sea ! no matter where the coast :
    The road that turns to home turns never wrong :
Where waves run high my bird will not be lost.
    His home I know : 'tis where the winds are strong ;
Where, on her throne of billows, rolling hoary
And green and blue and splashed with sunny glory,
Far, far from shore—from farthest promontory—
The mighty Mother sings the triumphs of her story,
      Sings to my bird the song !

THEODORE WATTS.

A COARSE MORNING.

Oh the yellow boisterous sea,
   The surging, chafing, murderous sea !
And the wind-gusts hurtle the torn clouds by,
On to the south through a shuddering sky,
And the bare black ships scud aloof from the land.
   'Tis as like the day as ever can be,
When the ship came in sight that came never to strand,
The ship that was blown on the sunken sand—
   And he coming back to me !

Oh the great white snake of foam,
   The coiling, writhing snake of white foam,
Hissing and huddering out in the bay,
Over the banks where the wrecked ship lay,
Over the sands where the dead may lie deep !
   There are some in the churchyard loam,
Some two or three the sea flung to our keep :
Their mothers can sit by a grave to weep,
   But *my* son never came home.

AUGUSTA WEBSTER.

ON THE SHORE.

THE angry sunset fades from out the west,
  A glimmering greyness creeps along the sea ;
Wild waves, be hushed, and moan into your rest,
  Soon will all earth be sleeping, why not ye ?

Far off, the heavens deaden o'er with sleep,
  The purple twilight darkens on the hill ;
Why will ye only ever wake and weep?
  I weary of your sighing, oh ! be still.

But ever, ever, moan ye by the shore,
  While all your trouble surges in my breast ;
Oh, waves of trouble, surge in me no more,
  Or be but still awhile and let me rest.

AUGUSTA WEBSTER.

THE FLOWING TIDE.

THE slow green wave comes curling from the bay,
  And leaps in spray along the sunny marge,
And steals a little more and more away,
  And drowns the dulse, and lifts the stranded barge.
Leave me, strong tide, my smooth and yellow shore ;
But the clear waters deepen more and more :
  Leave me thy pathway of the sands, strong tide ;
  Yet are the waves more fair than all they hide.

AUGUSTA WEBSTER.

SONG OF THE WATER-NIXIES.

By the ripple, ripple of the shallow sea,
      By the rocky sea,
      By the hollow sea,
We have built a giant windmill, with its long arms free,
      And it grinds, that we
      May not hungry be.
With a rumble and a roar, sounding all along the shore,
We should vanish and should perish if our wheel were
    heard no more.

Little hopes of fisher-maidens in the far-off town,
      In our wheel go down,
      Evermore go down,
For the fisher lads that hold them in the deep sea drown;
      By our grinding drown,
      For our pleasures drown.
Rend the garment from the soul; let it go, we care not
    where;
What do mortals want with spirit?   'Tis the bodies that
    are fair.

Out beyond the green horizon lurks the vengeful day,
      Lurks the fateful day,
      Lurks the hateful day,
When the winds shall cease to help us in our shark-like
    play,
      When our calm cold sway
      Shall have passed away,
When the wreckers and the wrecked both at peace shall
    be,—
When the threat shall be fulfilled, and there be no more
    sea.

SARAH WILLIAMS.

X

BALLADE OF SEA-MUSIC.

Sink, sun, in crimson far away,
  Float out, pale moon, above the roar,
While brown and silver, flame and grey,
  Round rock and sand the waters pour ;
  For night hath clue to all the store
Of wild wave-harmony that rings,
  And Earth hath not in all her lore
  Such legends as sea-music brings.

Here singing silver shallows fray
  The ruby tufted golden floor,
Here wondrous twilit forests sway
  Round coral porch and corridor
  Where lurk—but ah, why yet implore
The splendid dream that round them clings ? . .
  Where the dead lie who heard of yore
  The legends that sea-music brings.

This is the sea that could not stay
  The tides of men, that evermore
Rolled westward still and cleft its spray
  With hollowed trunk and dauntless oar :
  Here Grecian trireme reeled before
Rome's purple galley ; here sea-kings
  Left red on wave and blackened shore
  The legends that sea-music brings.

Envoy.

Earth keeps not now the face she wore ;
  The smoke-trails dusk the wide white wings ;
No longer as of old shall soar
  The legends that sea-music brings.

Mortimer Wheeler.

ADRIFT.

BEYOND the harbour bar the sun goes down
Into a bank of vapour rising brown,
  And thrusting shadowy arms into the sky ;
The church-vane glistens last in the grey town.

Seaward the waters run their scurrying race ;
Billows curl upward oftener with white face ;
  And that long streak where broken waves leap high
The limit of the ocean, nears apace.

The salt spray born of clashing wave and wave,
Anon a land-wind to the westward drave,
  And tangled beds of sea-weed drifted by,
And strong-winged sea-gulls through the spray-showers
    clave.

The last faint gleam dies off the steadfast vane ;
The risen vapour thickens into rain ;
  The sky stoops downward to the leaden sea,
Veiling the land.   Will he see land again ?

Drifting away upon the ebbing tide,
Oarless toward an ocean, opening wide
  Beyond the bar, o'er which even now in glee
Waves toss him.   Only God can be his guide.

Over the bar waves tumble fierce and hoar ;
Rude reaches stretch unto a far-off shore,
  And wandering tempests rage eternally ;
For him the sun shall smite the vane no more !

J. CHAPMAN WOODS.

IN front between the gaping heights
  The mystic ocean hung.

COVENTRY PATMORE.

TO watch the crisping ripples on the beach,
And tender curving lines of creamy spray.

LORD TENNYSON.

THE whole world and the sea that is
  In fashion like a chrysopras.

A. C. SWINBURNE.

AND the crest
Of every mounting wave is rimm'd with gold.

R. GARNETT.

THE WORLD BELOW THE BRINE.

THE world below the brine,
Forests at the bottom of the sea, the branches and leaves,
Sea-lettuce, vast lichens, strange flowers and seeds, the
    thick tangle, openings, and pink turf,
Different colours, pale grey and green, purple, white, and
    gold, the play of light through the water,
Dumb swimmers there among the rocks, coral, gluten,
    grass, rushes, and the aliment of the swimmers,
Sluggish existences grazing there suspended, or slowly
    crawling close to the bottom,
The sperm-whale at the surface blowing air and spray, or
    disporting with his flukes,
The leaden-eyed shark, the walrus, the turtle, the hairy
    sea-leopard, and the sting-ray,
Passions there, wars, pursuits, tribes, sight in those
    ocean-depths, breathing that thick-breathing air, as
    so many do,
The change thence to the sight here, and to the subtle air
    breathed by beings like us who walk this sphere,
The change onward from ours to that of beings who walk
    other spheres.

WALT WHITMAN.

AFTER THE SEA-SHIP.

AFTER the sea-ship, after the whistling winds,
Alter the white-grey sails taut to their spars and ropes,
Below, a myriad myriad waves hastening, lifting up their
　　necks,
Tending in ceaseless flow toward the track of the ship,
Waves of the ocean bubbling and gurgling, blithely
　　prying
Waves, undulating waves, liquid, uneven, emulous
　　waves,
Toward that whirling current, laughing and buoyant,
　　with curves,
Where the great vessel sailing and tacking displaced the
　　surface,
Larger and smaller waves in the spread of the ocean
　　yearnfully flowing,
The wake of the sea-ship after she passes, flashing and
　　frolicsome under the sun,
A motley procession with many a fleck of foam and many
　　fragments,
Following the stately and rapid ship, in the wake fol-
　　lowing.

WALT WHITMAN.

FROM "OUT OF THE CRADLE ENDLESSLY ROCKING."

ONCE Paumanok,
When the lilac-scent was in the air and the Fifth
      month grass was growing,
Up this sea-shore in some briers,
Two feather'd guests from Alabama, two together,
And their nest, and four light-green eggs spotted
      with brown,
And every day the he-bird to and fro near at hand,
And every day the she-bird crouch'd on her nest,
      silent, with bright eyes,
And every day I, a curious boy, never too close,
      never disturbing them,
Cautiously peering, absorbing, translating.

Shine ! shine ! shine !
Pour down your warmth, great sun !
While we bask, we two together.

Two together !
Winds blow south, or winds blow north,
Day come white, or night come black,
Home, or rivers and mountains from home,
Singing all time, minding no time,
While we two keep together.

Till of a sudden,
Maybe kill'd, unknown to her mate,
One forenoon the she-bird crouch'd not on her nest,
Nor return'd that afternoon, nor the next,

Nor ever appear'd again.
And thenceforward all summer in the sound of the sea,
And at night under the full of the moon in calmer weather,
Over the hoarse surging of the sea,
Or flitting from brier to brier by day,
I saw, I heard at intervals the remaining on, the he-bird
The solitary guest from Alabama.

Blow ! blow ! blow !
Blow up sea-winds along Paumanok's shore ;
I wait and I wait till you blow my mate to me.

Yes when the stars glisten'd,
All night long on the prong of a moss-scallop'd stake,
Down almost amid the slapping waves,
Sat the lone singer wonderful causing tears.

He call'd on his mate,
He pour'd forth the meanings which I of all men know.

Yes my brother I know,
The rest might not, but I have treasur'd every note,
For more than once dimly down to the beach gliding,
Silent, avoiding the moonbeam, blending myself with the
        shadows,
Recalling now the obscure shapes, the echoes, the sounds
        and sights after their sorts,
The white arms out in the breakers tirelessly tossing,
I with bare feet, a child, the wind wafting my hair,
Listen'd long and long.

Listen'd to keep, to sing, now translating the notes,
Following you my brother.

Soothe! soothe! soothe!
Close on its wave soothes the waves behind
And again another behind embracing and lapping, every·
one close,
But my love soothes not me, not me.

Low hangs the moon, it rose late,
It is lagging—O I think it is heavy with love, with love.

O madly the sea pushes upon the land
With love, with love.

O night! do I not see my love fluttering out among the
breakers!
What is that little black thing I see there in the white?

*   *   *   *   *   *

O brown halo in the sky near the moon, drooping upon
the sea!
O troubled reflection in the sea!
O throat! O throbbing heart!
And I singing uselessly, uselessly all the night.

*   *   *   *   *   *

The aria sinking,
All else continuing, the stars shining,
The winds blowing, the notes of the bird continuous
echoing,
With angry moans the fierce old mother incessantly
moaning,

Y

On the sands of Paumanok's shore grey and rustling,
The yellow half-moon enlarged, sagging down, drooping,
    the face of the sea almost touching,
The boy ecstatic, with his bare feet the waves, with his
    hair the atmosphere dallying,
The love in heart long pent, now loose, now at last tumul-
    tuously bursting,
The aria's meaning, the ears, the soul, swiftly depositing,
The strange tears down the cheeks coursing,
The colloquy there, the trio, each uttering,
The undertone, the savage old mother incessantly crying,
To the boy's soul's questions sullenly timing, some
    drown'd secret hissing,
To the outsetting bard.

Demon or bird ! (said the boy's soul,)
Is it indeed toward your mate you sing ? or is it really to
    me ?

   *   *   *   *   *   *   *

O give me the clue ! (it lurks in the night here some-
    where,)
O if I am to have so much, let me have more !

A word then, (for I will conquer it,)
The word final, superior to all,
Subtle, sent up—what is it ?—I listen ;

Are you whispering it, and have you been all the time,
    you sea-waves?
Is that it from your liquid rims and wet sands?
Whereto answering, the sea
Delaying not, hurrying not,
Whisper'd me through the night, and very plainly before
    daybreak,
Lisp'd to me the low and delicious word death,
And again death, death, death, death,
Hissing melodious, neither like the bird nor. like my
    arous'd child's heart,
But edging near as privately for me rustling at my feet
Creeping thence steadily up to my ears and laving me
    softly all over,
Death, death, death, death, death.

Which I do not forget,
But fuse the song of my dusky demon and brother,
That he sang to me in the moonlight on Paumanok's
    grey beach,
With the thousand responsive songs at random,
My own songs awaked from that hour,
And with them the key, the word up from the waves,
The word of the sweetest song and all songs,
That strong and delicious word which, creeping to my
    feet;
(Or like some old crone rocking the cradle, swathed in
    sweet garments, bending aside,)
The sea whisper'd me.

WALT WHITMAN.

Printed by WALTER SCOTT, Felling, Newcastle-upon-Tyne

The Canterbury Poets.

In SHILLING *Monthly Volumes. With Introductory Notices by* WILLIAM SHARP. MATHILDE BLIND. WALTER LEWIN. JOHN

ERRATA.

Page 71,
 line 1, should read,
  "Headlands stood out into the moon-lit deep."

Page 72,
 2nd Extract, line 3, should read,
  "Now swirling smoothly where the flat sand gave."
       and
 3rd Extract, line 2, should read,
"Its harvest of shell and seaweed that none or garners or reaps."

Page 90,
 line 1, delete comma after "suffered."
 line 4, last word should be "grown."
 line 12, comma after "which."

Page 118,
 1st verse, line 3, should read,
  "It lures me, lures me on to go."

Page 169, Longfellow,
 line 11 should be,
  "A rushing," &c., instead of "And rushing."

Page 225, Mary Robinson,
 verse 1, line 5, "sling" should be "slings."
 verse 2, line 9, "Gloom as of gather'd," &c., instead of "as *if.*"

  „ Lady of the Lake, etc. | **POETRY.**

 "Handy volumes, tastefully bound, and well finished in every respect."—*Pall Mall Gazette.*

London : WALTER SCOTT, 24 Warwick Lane, Paternoster Row.

Printed by WALTER SCOTT, Felling, Newcastle-upon-Tyne

The Canterbury Poets.

In SHILLING *Monthly Volumes. With Introductory Notices by* WILLIAM SHARP, MATHILDE BLIND, WALTER LEWIN, JOHN HOGBEN, A. J. SYMINGTON, JOSEPH SKIPSEY, EVA HOPE, JOHN RICHMOND, ERNEST RHYS, PERCY E. PINKERTON, MRS. GARDEN, DEAN CARRINGTON, DR. J. BRADSHAW, FREDERICK COOPER, HON. RODEN NOEL, J. ADDINGTON SYMONDS, ERIC MACKAY, G. WILLIS COOKE, ERIC S. ROBERTSON, WM. TIREBUCK, STUART J. REID, MRS. FREILIGRATH KROEKER, J. LOGIE ROBERTSON, M.A., SAMUEL WADDINGTON, etc.

Cloth, Red Edges	· 1s.	*Red Roan, Gilt Edges,*	2s. 6d.
Cloth, Uncut Edges ·	· 1s.	*Silk Plush, Gilt Edges,*	4s. 6d.

VOLUMES ALREADY ISSUED.

CHRISTIAN YEAR.
COLERIDGE.
LONGFELLOW.
CAMPBELL.
SHELLEY.
WORDSWORTH.
BLAKE.
WHITTIER.
POE.
CHATTERTON.
BURNS. Songs.
         „   Poems.
MARLOWE.
KEATS.
HERBERT.
VICTOR HUGO.
COWPER.
SHAKESPEARE:
   Songs, Poems, and Sonnets.
EMERSON.
SONNETS OF THIS CENTURY.
WHITMAN.
SCOTT. Marmion, etc.
    „   Lady of the Lake, etc.

PRAED.
HOGG.
GOLDSMITH.
ERIC MACKAY'S LOVE LETTERS, etc.
SPENSER.
CHILDREN OF THE POETS.
BEN JONSON.
BYRON (2 Vols.)
SONNETS OF EUROPE.
ALLAN RAMSAY.
SYDNEY DOBELL.
POPE.
HEINE.
BEAUMONT AND FLETCHER.
BOWLES, LAMB, AND HARTLEY COLERIDGE.
EARLY ENGLISH POETRY.

"Handy volumes, tastefully bound, and well finished in every respect."—*Pall Mall Gazette.*

London : WALTER SCOTT, 24 Warwick Lane, Paternoster Row.

The Camelot Series.

New Comprehensive Edition of Favourite Prose Works.
Edited by ERNEST RHYS.

In SHILLING Monthly Volumes, Crown 8vo ; each Volume containing from 300 to 350 pages, clearly printed on good paper, and strongly bound in Cloth.

VOLUMES ALREADY ISSUED.

ROMANCE OF KING ARTHUR.
By Sir THOMAS MALORY. Edited by ERNEST RHYS.

WALDEN. By H. THOREAU. Edited by W. H. DIRCKS.

CONFESSIONS OF AN ENGLISH OPIUM-EATER.
By THOMAS DE QUINCEY. Edited by W. SHARP.

LANDOR'S CONVERSATIONS. Edited by H. ELLIS.

PLUTARCH'S LIVES. With Introduction by B. J. SNELL.

SIR T. BROWNE'S RELIGIO MEDICI, Etc.
With Introduction by JOHN ADDINGTON SYMONDS.

ESSAYS AND LETTERS OF PERCY BYSSHE SHELLEY. With Introduction by ERNEST RHYS.

PROSE WRITINGS OF SWIFT.
With Introduction by WALTER LEWIN.

MY STUDY WINDOWS. By JAMES R. LOWELL.
With Introduction by RICHARD GARNETT, LL.D.

GREAT ENGLISH PAINTERS. By CUNNINGHAM.
With Introduction by WILLIAM SHARP.

LORD BYRON'S LETTERS. Edited by M. BLIND.

ESSAYS BY LEIGH HUNT. Edited by A. SYMONS.

LONGFELLOW'S PROSE WORKS.
Edited, with Introduction, by WILLIAM TIREBUCK.

GREAT MUSICAL COMPOSERS.
Edited, with Introduction, by Mrs. SHARP.

MARCUS AURELIUS. Edited by ALICE ZIMMERN.

SPECIMEN DAYS IN AMERICA. By WALT WHITMAN.

WHITE'S NATURAL HISTORY OF SELBORNE.
Edited, with Introduction, by RICHARD JEFFERIES.

DEFOE'S CAPTAIN SINGLETON.
Edited, with Introduction, by H. HALLIDAY SPARLING.

The Series is issued in two styles of Binding—Red Cloth, Cut Edges ; and Dark Blue Cloth, Uncut Edges. Either Style, 1s.

MONTHLY SHILLING VOLUMES.

GREAT WRITERS.

A New Series of Critical Biographies.

EDITED BY PROFESSOR E. S. ROBERTSON.

ALREADY ISSUED—

LIFE OF LONGFELLOW. By Professor ERIC S. ROBERTSON.

"The story of the poet's life is well told. . . . The remarks on Longfellow as a translator are excellent."—*Saturday Review.*

"No better life of Longfellow has been published."—*Glasgow Herald.*

LIFE OF COLERIDGE. By HALL CAINE.

The *Scotsman* says—"It is a capital book. . . . Written throughout with spirit and great literary skill. The bibliography is unusually full, and adds to the value of the work."

The *Academy* says—"It is gracefully and sympathetically written, . . . and it is no small praise to say it is worthy of the memory which it enshrines."

LIFE OF DICKENS. By FRANK T. MARZIALS.

"An interesting and well-written biography."—*Scotsman.*

LIFE OF DANTE GABRIEL ROSSETTI. By JOSEPH KNIGHT.

LIFE OF SAMUEL JOHNSON. By Col. F. GRANT.

LIFE OF DARWIN. By G. T. BETTANY.

CHARLOTTE BRONTË. By AUGUSTINE BIRRELL.

Ready July 25th.

LIFE OF THOMAS CARLYLE. BY RICHARD GARNETT, LL.D.

To be followed on August 25th by

LIFE OF ADAM SMITH. By R. B. HALDANE, M.P.

Volumes in preparation by AUSTIN DOBSON, WILLIAM ROSSETTI, WILLIAM SHARP, etc.

LIBRARY EDITION OF "GREAT WRITERS."

An Issue of all the Volumes in this Series will be published, printed on large paper of extra quality, in handsome binding, Demy 8vo, price 2s. 6d. per volume.

London: WALTER SCOTT, 24 Warwick Lane, Paternoster Row.

NOW READY.

Crown 8vo, Price 4s. 6d.

For
A Song's Sake

AND OTHER STORIES.

BY

THE LATE PHILIP BOURKE MARSTON

WITH A MEMOIR BY WILLIAM SHARP.

The Globe says :—" The volume should be acquired, if only for the sake of the memoir by Mr. William Sharp, by which it is prefaced. . . . The fullest and most authoritative account that has yet appeared. Its statements may be relied upon, it is excellent in feeling, and it affords altogether a successful portrayal of the poet."

The Scotsman says :—" A brief memoir by Mr. William Sharp, ably and sympathetically written, introduces the stories, and makes the volume one which the author's many admirers will be eager to possess. . . . Powerful studies, romantic in sentiment."

London : WALTER SCOTT, 24 Warwick Lane, Paternoster Row.

*Crown 8vo, 440 pages, printed on antique paper,
cloth gilt, price 3s. 6d.*

WOMEN'S
VOICES.

An Anthology of the most characteristic Poems

by English, Scotch, and Irish Women.

Selected, Arranged, and Edited

By Mrs. WILLIAM SHARP.

LONDON: WALTER SCOTT, 24 WARWICK LANE.

Uniform in size with " The Canterbury Poets," 365 pages.

Cloth Gilt, price 1s. 4d.

DAYS OF THE YEAR.

A POETIC CALENDAR

OF PASSAGES FROM THE WORKS OF

ALFRED AUSTIN.

Selected and arranged by A. S.

———

With an Introduction by WILLIAM SHARP.

———

"In a daintily-printed little volume, a friendly hand has brought together, from the poems of Mr. Alfred Austin, a complete Poetic Calendar for the Year. Each day has its separate flower of song fitting to the season, or true to the thoughts that the season suggests—a rosary for the daily devotions of those who love Nature and can feel the charm of verse. . . . To all who care for sweet thoughts sweetly expressed, who have mused in the green lanes of England, or watched storm and sunshine over English uplands ; to all who find melody and harmony in Nature, this daily remembrancer of things that they delight in cannot fail to be a welcome companion."—*Standard.*

London : **WALTER SCOTT, 24 Warwick Lane, Paternoster Row.**

The Canterbury Poets.

In Crown Quarto, Printed on Antique Paper,
Price 12s. 6d.

EDITION DE LUXE.

SONNETS OF THIS CENTURY.

With an Exhaustive and Critical Essay on the Sonnet,

BY WILLIAM SHARP.

This edition has been thoroughly Revised, and several
new Sonnets added.

A Special Edition of "Sonnets of this Century,"

On Whatman's Hand-made Paper, uncut edges, consisting of
FIFTY COPIES ONLY, consecutively numbered and signed,

AT 30/- EACH, NETT.

ONLY A FEW COPIES NOW LEFT.

THE VOLUME CONTAINS SONNETS BY

LORD TENNYSON.	EDWARD DOWDEN.
ROBERT BROWNING.	EDMUND GOSSE.
A. C. SWINBURNE.	ANDREW LANG.
MATTHEW ARNOLD.	GEORGE MEREDITH.
THEODORE WATTS.	CARDINAL NEWMAN.
ARCHBISHOP TRENCH.	*By the Late*
J. ADDINGTON SYMONDS.	DANTE GABRIEL ROSSETTI.
W. BELL SCOTT.	MRS. BARRETT-BROWNING.
CHRISTINA ROSSETTI.	C. TENNYSON-TURNER, etc.

AND ALL THE BEST WRITERS OF THE CENTURY.

London: WALTER SCOTT, 24 Warwick Lane, Paternoster Row

Now Ready, Price One Shilling; Post Free 1/2.

THE

Emigrant's Handbook

TO THE

British Colonies.

SUITABLE FOR EUROPEAN EMIGRATION.

Compiled by WALDEMAR BANNOW,

Author of " Guide to Emigration and Colonisation."

A BOOK EVERY BRITISH SUBJECT SHOULD READ.

London :

WALTER SCOTT, 24 Warwick Lane, Paternoster Row.

Price 6d.; Post Free, 7d.

No. I. READY SEPTEMBER 1st, 1887.

The Naturalists' Monthly:

A JOURNAL FOR NATURE-LOVERS AND NATURE-THINKERS.

EDITED BY Dr. J. W. WILLIAMS, M.A.

The Naturalists' Monthly will contain—

1. Original and Recreative Papers on Popular Scientific subjects by well-known writers.
2. Articles on the Distribution of Animal and Plant Life in the British Islands.
3. Monographs on groups generally looked over by the Field-Naturalist, as the British Fresh-water Worms and Leeches in Zoology, and the Lichens and Mosses in Botany.
4. Accounts of Scientific Voyages and Expeditions.
5. Biographical Lives of the Greatest Scientific Men.
6. "The Editor's Easy Chair"—a Monthly Chit-chat on the most important Scientific Questions of the day.
7. Reports of the Learned Societies.
8. General Notes and Correspondence.
9. Reviews of the latest Works and Papers.
10. Answer and Query Column for Workers.

The Naturalists' Monthly will be issued on the 1st of each Month.   Annual Subscription, 7/- post free.

London : WALTER SCOTT, 24 Warwick Lane, Paternoster Row.

The Camelot Series.

PRICE ONE SHILLING.

SPECIMEN DAYS

IN AMERICA.

BY WALT WHITMAN.

NEWLY REVISED BY THE AUTHOR, WITH FRESH
PREFACE AND ADDITIONAL NOTE.

London: WALTER SCOTT, 24 Warwick Lane, Paternoster Row

NEW BOOKS FOR CHILDREN.

———

Foolscap 8vo, Cloth Boards, price One Shilling each.

VERY SHORT STORIES

AND

VERSES FOR CHILDREN,

BY MRS. W. K. CLIFFORD,

Author of "Anyhow Stories," etc.

WITH AN ILLUSTRATION BY EDITH CAMPBELL.

———

A NEW NATURAL HISTORY

OF BIRDS, BEASTS, AND FISHES.

FOR THE YOUNG.

BY JOHN K. LEYS, M.A.

———

LIFE STORIES OF

FAMOUS CHILDREN.

ADAPTED FROM THE FRENCH.

By the Author of "Spenser for Children."

———

LONDON:

WALTER SCOTT, 24 Warwick Lane, Paternoster Row.

SEASON 1887.

Now Ready.   *Price (Cloth)* 3/6.

**THOROUGHLY REVISED, NEW ILLUSTRATIONS,
STEAMER TIME TABLES, SKELETON TOURS.**

The Land of the Vikings:

A POPULAR

GUIDE TO NORWAY.

London: WALTER SCOTT, 24 Warwick Lane, Paternoster Row.

www.ingramcontent.com/pod-product-compliance
Lightning Source LLC
Chambersburg PA
CBHW021748110726
47902CB00006B/1446